CHICAGO TANGO

CHICAGO TANGO

Tony Mankus

ISBN-13: 9781530438280
ISBN-10: 1530438284
Library of Congress Control Number: 2016904168
CreateSpace Independent Publishing Platform
North Charleston, South Carolina

CHAPTER 1

AURORA

Dennis Brunt followed Kevin Engstrom downstairs into Kevin's large basement. It was finished with paneled walls and had a bar and a tournament-size pool table, as well as a small gym. On the other side of the room there was also a fully equipped office, including a multimedia computer, a laser printer, a fax, and a phone with three landlines. The walls in the office were decorated with Princeton banners as well as large campaign posters showing Kevin in various photo opportunities. They looked professional; they were probably done by an advertising agency, Dennis surmised.

"My war room," Kevin remarked. "Are you interested in politics?"

"Not really," Dennis answered, although it was a soft no. He wondered whether Kevin was leading up to something. Dennis knew that Kevin had just entered the Republican primary race in the fourteenth congressional district of Illinois and was running against Joe Clayton, the incumbent.

"I'd like you and Linda to help out in the campaign," Kevin said, nodding to Dennis.

Linda, Kevin's younger sister, was a paralegal at the law office of Engstrom, Stackley, and Brunt, where Kevin and Dennis worked.

"I'm not really the political type," Dennis demurred.

"You'll do OK once you get the hang of it," Kevin said, putting a friendly arm around Dennis's shoulders. "Would you like a drink?"

"I'll take a Benedictine on the rocks," Dennis answered, examining the selection at the back of the bar.

Kevin walked behind the counter and started to prepare the drinks. "See if you can find some music," he said, nodding in the direction of the stereo.

Dennis sifted through the selection of CDs. He found one with Frank Sinatra and inserted it into the slot. The room filled with Frank's voice singing "A Foggy Day in London Town."

Dennis wasn't sure why Kevin and his wife Beverly had invited him to their home in Aurora, but since Kevin was the son of Morley Engstrom, the managing partner of Engstrom, Stackley, and Brunt, Dennis couldn't say no. He ran into Kevin regularly at the office, but the professional relationship hadn't crossed into a more personal one—at least until now. Maybe it had something to do with the fact that Dennis had recently started to date Linda.

"Clayton has most of the conservative votes here," Kevin went on, handing Dennis his drink. "He built up a sizable war chest with generous contributions from the local businesses."

Dennis took the tumbler with his drink and waited for Kevin to continue. Kevin was handsome in a boyish sort of way. He had a full head of black hair and, although the boyishness had started to fade as he neared forty, he was the kind of man who aged well, Dennis thought, like a TV news anchor.

"So our strategy is to go after the more moderate voters," Kevin said, clinking glasses with Dennis, "including women and Hispanics."

Dennis took a sip of his drink. The alcohol and the sugar gave him a quick buzz.

"Since you and Linda speak Spanish," Kevin went on, "maybe you guys can attend some local barbecues and birthday parties." The twinkle in Kevin's eyes got a little brighter. "Maybe you can taste some of the *lechones* and watch the kids break the *piñatas*."

Dennis didn't say anything. He decided to hold off from expressing any further skepticism.

"C'mon," Kevin said, changing the topic, "rack the balls."

Dennis took another swig of his drink and racked the balls with the triangle. Kevin picked out a cue stick and broke the rack. The balls scattered instantly with a crack, shooting out in all directions. They reminded Dennis of the pictures he'd seen recently in the *Chicago Tribune* about subatomic particle collisions in a nuclear accelerator. The article was about the experiments at Fermilab in Batavia. Some of the scientists there, it said, were looking for the Higgs boson, popularly known as "the God particle."

"I also want to talk to you about Gerhard Schmidt," Kevin said, rubbing the blue chalk cube on the tip of his cue stick. "Have you heard of him?"

"Can't say that I have," Dennis said, easing back into the present.

Kevin looked over the table and selected a shot. He curled the index finger of his left hand around the front of the cue stick and moved into position behind the white ball. His right hand held the end of the cue stick lightly as he aimed at the six ball and shot. The six ball lasered across the table and sank into the corner pocket with a solid clack. The white cue ball stopped momentarily at the point of impact, spinning in place like a squealing tire, and then rolled backward before coming to rest.

Kevin seemed pleased.

"He's an Argentinean businessman of German origin," he went on. "The US Attorney here in Chicago has begun to investigate his business dealings. The rumor is that Schmidt's involved in drug dealing, illegal arms trading, and money laundering."

"That's heavy stuff."

"He retained our law firm to represent him," Kevin said.

"Sounds like a big client," Dennis responded politely, although he didn't see how this had anything to do with him.

"My dad's known him for years. I think he's done some commercial work for Schmidt in the past. He'll give you a briefing on the case first thing Monday morning."

"A briefing?" Dennis became more alert. "He wants *me* to get involved in the case?"

"Yeah."

"I don't do criminal work," Dennis said, chalking the tip of his cue stick.

"He's also being investigated for tax evasion."

"That sounds like something Stackley would do. He usually takes the bigger cases."

"Gerhard asked for you specifically, as I understand," Kevin said, positioning himself for the next shot.

Dennis felt a jolt. A man he didn't know—a big shot—had asked for him by name. He wasn't sure how to respond to that. His mental wheels started to turn. Dennis wondered whether the fact that he had been born in Argentina had anything to do with it, but dismissed the seeming connection as too far-fetched. He left Argentina when he was only five years old, when he was adopted by Joe and Myrtle Brunt here in Chicago. He hadn't had any contact with Argentina since.

There was a pause in the conversation. Kevin examined the pool table for the next shot. Dennis heard Sinatra singing "Nancy (with the Laughing Face)."

"How does he know me?" Dennis asked.

"I don't know. Maybe Dad mentioned you to him."

Dennis's wheels started to turn again. Images—some long forgotten—appeared and disappeared in rapid succession, like a DVD on fast forward: his mother's face, an airplane, a flight attendant, a Teddy bear he'd gotten from Joe Brunt, his adoptive father, when he arrived at O'Hare. He shook off the images and focused back on the present.

Kevin took his next shot. The two ball zoomed straight across the table and sank into the side pocket. The cue ball stopped dead at the point of impact, as if it had been nailed with a hammer.

"But I would jump at the chance if I were you," Kevin said. "It's a hell of a big case. You do a good job, and it could mean a partnership for you, just like your dad's."

Dennis felt another jolt. He just had a partnership dangled before him by the son of the managing partner. Dennis didn't know how to respond. He reached up inside of his shirt and touched the silver medallion hanging around his neck. He'd never taken it off since he left Argentina, almost thirty years ago.

● ● ●

Linda and Dennis jumped into Kevin's SUV. She had volunteered to drive Dennis home. She backed the SUV out of the garage and headed toward his condo.

The streets were dark, other than the intermittent lights that illuminated the damp macadam. A slight drizzle added to the quiet gloominess of the evening. They were silent for a while, listening to the sizzle of the tires.

It was the middle of December. The drizzle would probably turn to snow as the temperature dropped into the night. Tiny white flakes were already beginning to mix in. Dennis's mind drifted to the conversation with Kevin and the new case he would be getting involved with. He felt uneasy about it.

"Have you heard of this guy Gerhard Schmidt?" Dennis asked, breaking the silence.

"I think he's a client of the law firm," Linda answered. "I've seen him around the office a few times."

Dennis remained silent, in thought.

"He must be something special," Linda went on. "You don't usually talk about your clients." Her comment was neutral, meant to encourage Dennis's train of thought.

"I'm just wondering how Schmidt knows me," Dennis pondered out loud.

"Maybe you're making a name for yourself already." Linda winked at Dennis.

"I doubt it." Dennis lightened up. "The only ones who remember my name are the bartender at Berghoff's and the Polish cleaning lady who sees me at the office when I work late. She seems to have taken a maternal interest in me."

Linda's lips curled into a hint of a smile. She found Dennis's self-deprecating sense of humor charming. "Well, this might be a good opportunity for you to *make* a name for yourself," she reassured him.

Those were almost the exact same words Kevin used, Dennis thought. He glanced back at Linda, wondering if she intended some sort of double entendre. His mind wandered off again. He had an uneasy feeling that there were some missing pieces in this puzzle.

"You seem a little tense," Linda said, turning slightly toward him. "Would you like to stop at my place for a drink?"

That was a clear invitation. It meant spending the night with her, if the past was any indication.

"Sure," he answered. He was always up for making love. Besides, saying yes was easier than trying to figure out the bigger things that seemed to be going on. "I think I could use another drink," he added.

They pulled into the parking lot of Linda's condo and took the elevator to the fourth floor. She leaned closer and kissed him in the silent intimacy of a moving elevator. Her perfume was alluring. He felt himself beginning to relax, the first time all day—the first time in the last several weeks, maybe.

The elevator door opened. They walked hand in hand to the door of her condo. He thought about Kevin's offer to get them involved in his campaign.

"Did Kevin mention anything to you about us campaigning for him?" he asked.

"Yes, he did," Linda said, taking the door keys out of her purse. "He wants us to campaign for him in the Hispanic community."

"I suppose it makes sense. We both speak Spanish. The only thing is, I didn't think there were many Hispanics in this district."

"You'd be surprised," she said, unlocking the door.

"I guess I would be, although most of them must be illegal."

"A lot of them are."

They walked into the apartment. Linda slipped out of her coat and hung it in the closet. She was dressed in a white blouse, a red skirt that stopped just above the knees, and matching high-heeled shoes. She looked incredibly sexy, Dennis thought. Linda noticed his admiring glance and kissed him again. He brushed his fingers through her lush, auburn hair. With the high heels, she was almost his height.

"Would you like to fix some drinks for us?" she asked, taking his coat. "I'll take a red wine."

Dennis picked up a bottle of Merlot from the wine rack along with two glasses while Linda rummaged through her collection of CDs. She found one with Tony Bennett's all-time hits. The rich sound of violins, backed by a full orchestra, filled the room as Tony's youthful voice sang "Because of You."

"What doesn't make sense to me is why Kevin is going after the Hispanic vote," Dennis wondered out loud, picking up the thread of the conversation. "Illegal immigrants don't vote."

"No, they don't," Linda said, sitting down on the couch in the living room. "But the Hispanic community is a growing influence. I don't know if you've seen the demographics."

"No, I haven't."

"Well, I have. Their numbers are increasing and their media is becoming quite influential."

"Yeah, but what does that do for Kevin's campaign?"

"Favorable coverage in the Hispanic media can have a spillover effect."

Dennis uncorked the fresh bottle of wine and poured some into each glass. "Spillover into what?" he asked.

"Into the mainstream media. The American media pays attention to the Hispanic media. If they see that Kevin's getting a lot of play there, they're going to wonder what he's up to."

Dennis recorked the bottle, picked up the glasses, and walked over to Linda.

"Well, here's to your brother's successful campaign," he said, offering to clink glasses. Linda touched the lip of her glass with his and took a sip.

"It tastes good," she said, smiling at him. Her smile seemed inviting.

Dennis sat down next to her, swung his feet over the edge of the couch, and started to lie back, aiming his head toward Linda's lap. He extended his arm with the glass of wine delicately through this semi acrobatic maneuver in an effort to keep it gravitationally balanced. He didn't spill a drop.

"Nice move," Linda commented, raising her glass in the air to accommodate his shift.

Tony Bennett started into "Who Can I Turn To." It was one of Dennis's favorites. For a moment he listened quietly to the heart-wrenching lyrics of Anthony Newley, matched perfectly by Bennett's tenor voice and the lush sound of the full orchestra. The wine and the music, together with Linda's perfume, were a powerful combination. The guard he always kept up began to slip. He started to let go—but not completely.

Dennis thought about his relationship with Linda. She was in her early thirties already, past the blush of youth, but still attractive. She had been married once, but the marriage had collapsed. The divorce was finalized after only twenty months. There were no children and the parting was relatively friendly. She'd joined the Peace Corps after that and spent two years in Ecuador, before returning to Chicago and joining her dad and brother as a paralegal in their law firm.

Dennis liked her, but he didn't think he was in love with her. He wasn't sure what love was. He dated often before he met Linda, but never seemed to form any long-term relationships. Maybe he just enjoyed being with her. She took him around to meet people—something he wouldn't do on his own. Making love to her was exquisite; he would've done it every day—several times a day, maybe.

He took another sip of wine and looked up at Linda. She sighed and touched his lips with her fingers. Dennis felt a strong desire to take her in his arms, to envelop her in his embrace. He set the glass down on the floor and sat up. Linda's half-full glass dropped to the carpet as she lay back on the couch. His hands slipped under her skirt and found their way under the elastic band of her panties. Linda's open lips crushed against his as he faded into a trance of perfume, perspiration, and auburn hair.

The sexual desire he felt for her was irresistible, like the power of an ocean wave. Dennis wanted to have her, more than anything in the world. He wanted all of her.

CHAPTER 2

ENGSTROM, STACKLEY, AND BRUNT

Dennis took the Northwestern express train from Aurora to Chicago for the meeting with Schmidt. Once he arrived at Union Station, it was a short walk to the law firm's downtown office on Wacker Drive. He usually enjoyed it if it was a nice day, like today: a brisk but brilliantly sunny December morning, about ten days before Christmas. His steps had an extra bounce as he thought about what he was going to do for the holidays. He hadn't made any plans yet, but there was a lot of buzz about it this year. It was 1999, the end of the millennium, and people were speculating that something miraculous—or maybe cataclysmic—was going to happen.

The elevator whisked him up to the twenty-fifth floor. He walked in through the familiar double doors, next to the glass wall with the prominent logo proclaiming "Engstrom, Stackley & Brunt, Ltd."

"Your meeting is about to start," Kelli, the receptionist, greeted him. "In the conference room," she added, nodding to her right. "Would you like your usual cup of tea?"

"Yes, with extra lemon and honey on the side. Thanks, Kelli."

The spacious conference room was dominated by a large oval table and leather-cushioned chairs. Several people were seated already, including Norm Stackley, partner and senior tax attorney; Shaun Williams, the criminal attorney; and Enrico Monzoni, the investigator and computer guru. They all had mugs of coffee with the law-firm logo; Williams was eating a donut.

"Come in," Stackley motioned to Dennis. "Have a seat."

Dennis sat down in the empty swivel chair between Williams and Monzoni. He liked working with both of them, especially Enrico. Everybody called him Rico. He was six four and weighed 240 pounds, most of it muscle. Dennis regularly saw him and Shaun at the East Bank Health Club. Rico could bench-press 350 pounds. A second-generation Argentinean of Italian descent, he started out his adult life as an electrical engineer with IBM. He didn't like working for a large organization and quit to head up the technical support unit at Engstrom, Stackley, and Brunt, where he became interested in investigative work, especially in criminal matters. It dovetailed well with his computer skills and the love of guns that he'd inherited from his father. Rico was a licensed private investigator and owned dozens of guns registered in his name. He loved to show them to his friends and explain their workings and history.

"Which rod are you carrying today?" Dennis asked Rico, patting his jacket lapel. He was still in a bouncy mood.

"He's got a Luger," Shaun joked, picking up on Dennis's mood, "in honor of the occasion."

Shaun was another interesting character. He was one of the few black attorneys at the law firm. At thirty-seven he was fairly young to be heading up the criminal-law section, but his experience was rock solid. After graduating from Brown University and the University of Chicago Law School, he'd landed a job with the US Attorney's office in Chicago. He liked criminal work, but didn't like the prosecuting end of it, especially since many of the cases involved large businesses and white-collar crimes. He was more sympathetic to the underdog, the guy who got screwed by *the man*, as he liked to say.

He left the US Attorney's office after a few years and started his own practice with another African American attorney. They started out doing criminal defense work, mostly small DUI, drug and sexual offender cases, but built up a good reputation after successfully handling several high-profile federal cases through the federal indigent criminal defendants program. They didn't earn a lot in legal fees to begin with, but the media coverage helped. After that, they didn't have to work very hard to attract clients.

Shaun split from his partner and joined Engstrom, Stackley, and Brunt when he was offered a substantial increase in pay and the freedom to choose the types of cases he wanted to work. It was a win-win situation for both Shaun and the law firm. Morley Engstrom was shrewd enough to know that he would score some political points with the American Bar Association and the federal bench by increasing diversity, but he also knew that Shaun would help the bottom line by bringing in clients the law firm would not have attracted otherwise.

Kelli brought in the tea. Dennis squeezed in the lemon and poured in some honey. "What do I need to know about this case?" he asked.

"The US Attorney's office has started to investigate Schmidt and his business interests," Williams answered. "They've already issued several subpoenas."

"Has there been an indictment yet?" Dennis asked, stirring the tea with the silver teaspoon.

"Not yet," Williams answered, "but we have to be ready."

"You're going to head up the tax end of this," Stackley interjected. "We have to see where Schmidt is vulnerable and what we can do about mitigating any exposure."

The private door at the end of the conference room opened and Morley Engstrom walked in, followed by a man in his early sixties.

It must be Gerhard Schmidt, Dennis surmised. The man was dressed neatly in a dark-blue suit with a canary-yellow shirt and a red tie with thin, black stripes running diagonally. The triangular end of a canary-yellow handkerchief was visible from the breast pocket. He had wavy, black hair with gray sideburns. He appeared to be in good physical shape, though his skin seemed pale and had several small liver spots. Dennis couldn't get over the feeling that he knew Schmidt somehow.

"Gentlemen," Engstrom said, turning to the group, "this is Gerhard Schmidt. He's a long-term client who is being investigated by the US Attorney. This law firm and its full resources will be mobilized to help him."

Schmidt remained standing, but didn't say anything.

"Mr. Schmidt, I want you to meet the team assigned to your case. You've already met Shaun Williams, the lead criminal attorney. To his right is Dennis Brunt, the tax attorney. To his left is Enrico Monzoni, the investigator and computer guru who will help us gather any evidence that might be needed. Of course, you already know Norm Stackley, one of our senior partners."

They nodded in turn as they were introduced. Schmidt sat down without speaking. His demeanor was unassuming; he seemed almost diminutive against the leather backrest of his chair.

Engstrom lit a cigar and continued. "I hear from my sources that Brian Hannigan has opened an investigation on Mr. Schmidt. The lead attorney on the case is Phil Klein, but I understand that Hannigan is taking a personal interest. He sees this as a high-profile case that will provide him with ample media exposure—exposure he doesn't have to pay for in his campaign for governor."

Engstrom took a few puffs on the cigar. "Williams, you'll head up the team and develop the defense strategies. You'll also handle all the media and do any interviews when this gets out to the public. Public opinion is important in a high-profile case like this, but I would be judicious as to when and how often you grant interviews."

Engstrom glanced at Williams. Williams nodded.

Engstrom turned to Dennis. "Brunt, you'll have to go through a lot of the paperwork and computer files to see how much exposure Gerhard has. Hannigan has subpoenaed many of the records related to Gerhard's companies here in the US. He still hasn't gotten to his companies in Brazil, Argentina, and other Latin American countries, at least not that we know of."

Dennis shifted uneasily, but nodded.

"In order to get those files, Hannigan will need to go through the formal channels established through the tax treaties," Engstrom continued, "including the Competent Authority. That takes time, although I'm sure he has other sources available to him, including the CIA, DEA, and other agencies that have people at our embassies in those countries. So we'll need for you and Monzoni to fly down to Buenos Aires right away, where Gerhard has his headquarters."

That solves my Christmas agenda, Dennis thought, *or lack thereof.*

"Are you with me?" Engstrom barked gruffly at Dennis.

"Yes sir," Dennis shot back quickly. His habit of fading in and out of conversations got him in trouble at times.

"Kelli will get plane tickets and hotel reservations for both of you." Engstrom chomped on his cigar. "I'm hoping…"

Engstrom stopped speaking as Schmidt shifted slightly in his chair. "That won't be necessary," Schmidt spoke in a soft voice. "I'll make my private plane available," he added. His demeanor changed very little.

"Well, that takes care of the basic transportation issues," Engstrom continued. "As I was saying, I'm hoping to get the two of you out there within three or four days."

"Yes sir," Dennis repeated, nodding his head for good measure.

"That'll be all for now," Engstrom concluded, taking the cigar out of his mouth.

Everyone stood up to leave. Schmidt leaned over and whispered something to Engstrom.

"Brunt!" Engstrom called to Dennis. "Stay for a few minutes."

Dennis turned back and looked at Engstrom. He motioned Dennis to come over.

"Gerhard wants to have a few words with you in private," Engstrom said, pointing to his own chair. "Have a seat here. I'm going back to my office."

Dennis approached Schmidt cautiously.

"Please," Schmidt nodded, "sit down."

Dennis eased into the chair, but felt uncomfortable. As an attorney who helped clients with tax problems, he was used to being in control. They were usually stressed out and unsure of how to handle the situation, like patients going in for surgery. This felt different. Schmidt seemed to know more about Dennis than Dennis knew about him.

"Your main contact person in Buenos Aires will be Esmeralda Atoche," Schmidt said, looking at Dennis. "She is in charge of my day-to-day operations in Latin America."

Schmidt waited for Dennis to acknowledge that he understood. Dennis nodded without speaking.

"I trust her completely. She will show you everything you need to see."

Dennis nodded again.

"Be careful of Hector Torres, however," Schmidt continued. "He has ambitions beyond running the *estancia*, my ranch in the countryside. Please contact me if you have any trouble. I will make sure you are safe."

Dennis wondered what he was getting himself into.

"Also, Mr. Monzoni is going with you," Schmidt said, sensing Dennis's uneasiness. "He is, what you call, street smart. He will take good care of you."

Dennis nodded and stood up. He hesitated for a second, wondering if he should ask Schmidt what was going on.

"Do you have any questions?" Schmidt asked.

"Yes. Why do you want me involved in this case? I don't do criminal work."

"I want you to learn about my operations," Schmidt replied patiently.

"Why?" Dennis was still standing as if to leave, but turned slightly to face Schmidt. He wanted a straight answer.

"You will help to defend me better." Schmidt's answer seemed straightforward, but Dennis felt as though Schmidt was still holding back.

"You also speak Spanish," Schmidt went on. "That is important when you are investigating in Buenos Aires."

"That's it? You want me because I speak Spanish?" Dennis asked incredulously. "There must be hundreds of criminal attorneys in Chicago who speak Spanish."

Schmidt paused, then looked directly at Dennis. "I also want you to see your mother," he said. "Your *real* mother," he added.

Dennis's jaw dropped. He couldn't speak for a few seconds. He hadn't seen or spoken to his mother since he had left Argentina twenty-eight years before.

"My mother?" he blurted out. "What does she have to do with this?"

"She is in Argentina. You will see her when you go there. You wish to see her, do you not?"

"Of course I want to see her. I haven't seen her in almost thirty years."

"You will see her if you help me with this case."

Dennis didn't know what to say. "Where is she?" he asked finally. "Is she OK?"

"Yes, she is fine. You will be taken to her after you arrive in Buenos Aires."

Schmidt's answers were perfunctory, almost condescending. They conveyed very little real information. Dennis wanted to know more, but hesitated. He didn't want to make a rooky mistake with a big client of the law firm.

"How do you know her?" he ventured.

"She and I know each other from long ago," Schmidt continued in a non-committal tone.

"That's not a real answer."

"We will have accommodations for you and Mr. Monzoni in one of our apart hotels in Buenos Aires. I will also provide you with my personal cell phone number as soon as my new satellite telephones arrive. You will be able to contact me day or night."

Dennis's mind faded out of the present. It flashed back to the last time he saw his mother all those years ago. It was late December, just about this time of the year. He was five. She hung a silver St. Christopher medallion around his neck and kissed him. Tears ran down her cheeks as she told him that she loved him and asked him to never, ever forget her.

Dennis remembered the confusion he felt at that moment. "*Where am I going?*" he asked her. "*Why are you crying?*"

He remembered being put on a plane and looking out the window at her as she stood on the tarmac waving to him. After the plane soared above the clouds into the vastness of the blue sky, he cried silently, eyes closed. Dennis also thought about his older brother, Marko. He wished Marko were with him. Marko always looked out for him.

Then a pretty flight attendant came by and tried to console him. She brought him a Coke and some nuts. Later she came back with a breakfast of eggs, sausages, and toast with jelly. He remembered touching the silver medallion his mother gave him and promising the flight attendant that he wouldn't cry anymore.

Dennis shook himself back to the present. He glanced briefly at Schmidt to see whether he had anything else to say, but Schmidt's face had lost all expression. The slight glimmer in his eyes was gone. Dennis stood up to leave.

"Thank you for agreeing to take this case," Schmidt said, extending his hand. "I hope you will be able to help."

Dennis reached out to shake Schmidt's hand. "I hope so too," he said, diplomatically. Schmidt's hand felt cold.

CHAPTER 3

MOOSEHEAD LODGE

"**T**eamwork," Brian Hannigan said, looking at the small group scattered around the fireplace of the social room at Moosehead Lodge in northern Wisconsin. "That's what it takes."

Hannigan projected the relaxed and casual attitude of someone who was confident of his authority. He wanted to make it clear, though, that they hadn't gathered for a social occasion.

"We've got a job to do," he said, pointing his finger at them, "and the only way to do it—the only way *I* know how to do it—is through teamwork."

The emphasis on the "I" wasn't lost on his listeners. They were silent and attentive. The newer ones were intimidated. Those who'd been with him for a while knew him well enough to recognize that he was in his "leadership mode" and that they'd better *look* as though they were paying attention. Hannigan was a master of office politics and knew how to make life miserable—in subtle but unmistakable ways—for the underlings who dared to challenge his authority.

Hannigan spoke at a measured pace, pausing between sentences while keeping his gaze on his audience. The popping of the air bubbles from the dry cedar logs burning in the fireplace accentuated the pauses. It was a technique he'd picked up from Digger Phelps, his college basketball coach, and Phelps's locker room pep talks. The coach had a strong influence on Hannigan, not the least of which was the fact that he'd led them to the NCAA's "Elite Eight" in 1979, Hannigan's senior year at Notre Dame.

"And the job we have is to nail Gerhard Schmidt."

Pause.

"There's a short window of opportunity. We need to get enough evidence against Schmidt before he leaves the country."

Another pause.

"Our agents are tailing him twenty-four seven. If he tries to leave, we'll arrest him. We'll charge him with jaywalking if we have to. He's a high-priority target. Do I make myself clear?"

It was a rhetorical question, of course; he didn't want any answers, he wanted the group's attention. That wasn't too difficult. Besides his assertive tone and his outgoing "Type A" personality, Hannigan stood at six feet five, had good looks, and was physically fit. He was forty-two, in the prime of his life, although he could easily have passed for thirty-five.

"So I need some extra effort here," he continued. "I didn't become the US Attorney for the Northern District of Illinois to settle for anything less than full and complete commitment from my team."

Donna Stevens took another bite of her turkey and lettuce sandwich and washed it down with a swig from a can of Diet Coke. She hadn't eaten since she left Chicago after lunch for the drive to Wisconsin. She checked her watch. It was eight in the evening already. She glanced over to Roman Kaminski, one of the FBI agents assigned to this case. Roman gave her a friendly nod of acknowledgement, as if to say, "*Yup, he's on a roll.*"

Donna was one of the Assistant US Attorneys assigned to this case. She had formed a friendly working relationship with Roman. Donna liked Roman's unpretentiousness, his down-to-earth common sense, and his general congeniality. A second-generation Polish American, he was the first in his family to go to college. The GI Bill allowed him to do that after he finished a hitch in the Marine Corps. He had two young children with his lovely wife and liked to share their pictures with Donna.

This gig at the lodge wasn't common for the US Attorney's office in Chicago. Government agencies frowned at authorizing any expenditure for events that could be seen as nonessential. Hannigan used his personal funds to reserve this off-duty weekend at the Moosehead Lodge and hired a motivational team-building consultant company, Team Concepts, to head the retreat. Officially speaking, attendance was "voluntary" for everyone working on the Schmidt case, but most of them knew better than to make other plans for the weekend.

The scheduled team activities included building a wooden bridge to cross a brook, climbing a rock with the use of ropes and pulleys, and falling backward while blindfolded into the arms of another team member. Individual meetings were held throughout the day to discuss team members' experiences and evaluate their performances. Optional activities included using the firing range for target practice and going on a deer-hunting trip with bows and arrows.

"At this point," Hannigan continued, "I'd like to have Phil Klein give us a brief synopsis of what we know, or suspect, about Schmidt."

Klein ambled up to the front of the room, near the fireplace. He was only five feet eight and looked small next to Hannigan, but he had a muscular frame and a no-nonsense air about him that commanded respect, if not admiration. He wore a dark plaid logger's shirt over his broad shoulders and a yarmulke on his head. Hannigan had chosen Klein to head up the Schmidt case because of Klein's background.

Klein was an Orthodox Jew who lived in Skokie, in the northern suburbs of Chicago, with his wife and six children. After graduating from NYU, he volunteered for the Israeli army, where he saw combat as a tank commander. He met and married his wife there and lived a year on a kibbutz before they moved to Hyde Park in Chicago so he could attend the University of Chicago Law School. His paternal grandparents, who had lived in a ghetto in Vilnius, Lithuania, were murdered with other Jews when the Germans occupied Lithuania in 1941.

Before he became US Attorney for the Northern District of Illinois, Hannigan had worked with Klein at the US Justice Department's Office of Special Investigations, which focused on rooting out and deporting US residents who had participated in some way in the Holocaust. That was where Hannigan first became aware of Gerhard Schmidt and some of his illicit activities.

"The evidence we have so far," Klein began, "points to drug dealing, illegal arms trading, and money laundering. Schmidt's main operations are headquartered in Buenos Aires, but he seems to have expanded into other parts of Latin America, as well as the United States and Canada. Among other things, we are looking at tax evasion."

"What do we know about his background?" Hannigan asked.

"Schmidt's father, Klaus, was a high-ranking Nazi officer and SS member," Klein explained. "He escaped from Germany after the Second World War through the Odessa ratline, leaving his German wife and children behind. He settled in Argentina, changed his last name, and married an Argentinean woman. He continued to maintain ties with other Nazis in Argentina, however, and formed illegal business ventures with them and with corrupt officers in the Argentine military. Simon Wiesenthal's organization got on his track, but Klaus died before they could nail him."

"Did Gerhard Schmidt have any connections to his father's operations?" Hannigan asked.

"He took over all of his father's operations, as far as we know, changed his last name back to his father's German surname, and expanded the operations to an international scale. Along the way, Schmidt consolidated his power by eliminating some of his and his father's cohorts."

The people in the room, including the veterans, had grown silent. Satisfied with the impact, Hannigan stepped back to the front of the room.

"Thank you, Phil," he said, putting his hand on Klein's shoulder. "That'll be all for this evening." Hannigan turned to the group. "Before we break, though, I'm going to have George Petrakis, the head of Team Concepts, give you details of the schedule this weekend, as well as the rules and procedures here. Are there any questions as to why we're here and what's expected of you?"

Roman glanced at Donna and raised his hand.

"Roman!" Hannigan barked, pointing to Kaminski.

"I was wondering, Mr. Hannigan, whether we could use the firing range this evening?"

"I don't see why not," Hannigan answered, turning to Petrakis. "We've got lights here, don't we?"

Petrakis nodded. "We'll turn them on," he said.

"Just remember," Hannigan added, "we get started at six tomorrow morning, sharp! So don't get carried away with any extracurricular activities tonight."

After the briefing by Petrakis, the meeting broke up. Some headed for their rooms; others turned on the TV in the social room and helped themselves to snacks from the kitchen. Roman and Donna headed for the firing range. Roman pulled out a silver flask from the inside pocket of his jacket and offered it up to Donna.

"Care to have a nip?" he asked.

"Don't mind if I do," Donna said, taking it from Roman. She unscrewed the top and took several swallows. The sting of alcohol in her mouth was followed by a mellow glow that eased through her body.

"It's not very ladylike," she said, handing the flask back to Roman, "but it sure hits the spot."

That's what Roman liked about Donna—she was a lady who could let her hair down and have some fun without losing her class. Donna was an only child of a financial analyst and professional violinist. She was raised in Winnetka and graduated from Northwestern Law School, with honors. She was a member of the law review group in her senior year and was also on a team of students who helped a law professor free a black man from death row after he was wrongfully convicted for murder. She was somewhat liberal in her political outlook, especially as it related to women's issues, although lately she had begun to question the direction of her life.

"Here's mud in your eye," Roman said, taking a long quaff of the vodka. Donna counted at least four or five bobbles of his Adam's apple.

"Or, as my grandfather used to say," Roman declared, handing the flask back to Donna, "*Na zdrowie!*"

"I'm good," Donna said. "Thanks."

Roman put the flask back inside his jacket as they walked to the outdoor firing range, several hundred yards away.

"Maybe I'm not too bright," Roman continued, "but all this speech-making and motivational stuff gives me a headache."

"I try not to let it bother me," Donna replied, keeping pace with Roman.

"I heard rumors that Hannigan's running for the Governor of Illinois. Is that what this is about?"

"It's more than a rumor," Donna informed Roman. "He's already formed a committee of influential friends and wealthy donors."

"So it's a sure thing?"

"Not a hundred percent yet, but they're laying the groundwork for him. The only question is whether he's going to run as a Democrat or a Republican."

"An Irishman running as a Republican?" Roman muffled a laugh.

"That's just it. His roots are Democratic, but his politics are definitely conservative. He wouldn't have gotten this job if they weren't."

Roman nodded. "I guess this Schmidt case will be another feather in his political cap."

"You bet. He's counting on getting a lot of media attention from it."

They entered one of the stalls in the back of the firing range. "I don't blame Hannigan for trying to nail Schmidt," Roman said, picking up several sets of earmuffs. "I'm just saying I could do without this rah-rah stuff." He handed one set to Donna.

"His management style can be annoying at times," Donna concurred.

"Me, I'm a hands-on guy," Roman went on, taking out a pistol from a holster just below his left armpit. "I need something tangible."

He pressed the magazine release at the bottom of the grip and pulled out the clip. Satisfied that it was full, he pushed it back in and clicked it locked.

"It helps keep me in touch with reality."

He placed the earmuffs on his head and took aim at the target, a life-size image of a man with a scowl on his face. The shots rang out and popped squarely into the target's forehead.

"Maybe it's in my genes," Roman said, extending the handle of the gun carefully in Donna's direction. "My grandfather became a bricklayer after he got out of the war, just like his father. You lay the bricks one on top of the other. And when you're done, you can see the finished product."

Donna took the gun from Roman and examined it. It appeared to be a .40 caliber Beretta, a semiautomatic. She had handled guns during several trials and knew how some of them worked, but she'd never actually used one. She'd been thinking of getting one for herself. She lived alone in Chicago, in the Streeterville section, and her parents were concerned about her safety. Between robbers, rapists, and criminals she had helped put away, they thought it might be prudent to have one.

"Give it a try," Roman encouraged her.

Donna took aim at the target and squeezed the trigger. The recoil jolted her arm up above her head and she missed badly. She felt a tinge of ego rise to the surface. Roman was too much of a gentleman to smile, but she couldn't let him think she was a total wuss. She refocused and squeezed again. The second shot was better. It hit near the top of the target.

She removed the earmuffs and handed the pistol back to Roman.

"Good job," Roman said, taking the pistol from her. "A little more practice and you could get pretty good at it."

"I'm not sure I want to get any better at it," Donna said, hanging up her earmuffs. "I don't think my heart's in it."

Roman sensed Donna's mood and reached for the flask again. Donna took a few swallows before handing it back to Roman. She could feel the relaxing buzz lighten her mood.

"What *is* your heart into these days?" Roman asked.

Roman and Donna got along pretty well, but it was more of an office friendship; they didn't mingle socially. Her social set included the family friends from the North Shore, her college and law school friends, and her attorney acquaintances. His were more the law enforcement types and ethnic Polish from the Northwest side of Chicago. But the setting and the drinks gave him a cautious opening, he felt, to creep past that unspoken barrier.

"I'm not sure," Donna mused. "I seem to be losing my enthusiasm for prosecutorial work."

Roman took out a pack of cigarettes and offered one to her. Donna rarely smoked, but reached out to take one. Roman held up the polished metal lighter with the US Marine Corps insignia and let the flame singe the tip of Donna's cigarette. She took some puffs to get the embers going.

"I don't know," Donna continued. "Maybe I'll switch to a legal aid agency. The pay is terrible, but maybe I'll be helping someone who really needs it."

Roman took a puff from his own cigarette and inhaled deeply, the way he did when the buzz he got from alcohol gave him that first sense of well-being.

"I did all the right things," Donna went on. "I went to the right schools; I followed the path I thought was the right one. But now that I'm in the—quote—'real world,' it seems like something is lacking." She raised both hands at the "real world" phrase and gestured the quotation marks with her fingers.

"What's missing?" Roman asked with a trace of a smile. "You've got a nice family and a good job; you make good money. I could get used to that."

"I know. It sounds like I'm ungrateful. I've led a privileged life and I'm grateful for that. But everything seems so predictable, so structured."

"What's so predictable and structured about putting the bad guys behind bars?"

"That part's OK," Donna nodded. "But it seems like there is so much more out there than chasing the bad guys."

"Like what?" Roman asked. He sensed that Donna was on a roll.

"When you see the poverty in underdeveloped countries," Donna took another puff, "the cruelty of war, of ethnic cleansing, of abuse against women, you begin to question the meaning of what you're doing."

"Whoa!" Roman let out with animation. "That's heavy stuff."

"I know, but it seems like that's what I'm thinking about these days."

"Those problems have been around for a long time, Donna. Do you think you can really change them?"

"I don't know."

"Maybe it's my simple Polack perspective," Roman said, taking another puff of his cigarette, "but it seems like you could use a good man and kids to settle you down. Any 'significant other'—as they say—in your life?"

"No." Donna cracked a mild grin for the first time. "It seems like most of the good ones I knew got married while I was pursuing my career."

At this point, Hannigan and Klein walked into the firing range. They seemed in a jovial mood. Hannigan put his arm around Klein's shoulder and announced with a friendly smile that Klein wanted to take some target practice.

"Roman," Hannigan called out, "why don't you lend Phil your pistol. I want to see what he can do."

Roman took out his pistol and handed it to Klein. Klein checked the cartridge, released the safety, and fired off seven rounds. Six of them hit the target squarely in the face.

Hannigan let out a whistle. "Where in the hell did you learn to shoot like that?"

"Kibbutz," Klein said, handing the pistol back to Roman. He hadn't bothered with the earmuffs.

Roman put the Beretta back in its holster.

"A few other things," Hannigan said, addressing Donna and Roman, drawing them and Klein into a smaller circle. "I want you guys to fly out to Buenos Aires. Schmidt has his operations centralized there and I want you to nose around to see what you can find out. For one thing, I want to know why Schmidt is here in Chicago. Buzz Bixby, the ambassador there, as well as his staff, should be of some help to you."

Donna and Roman perked up. That seemed like an interesting development.

"And another thing," Hannigan went on, "I want you guys to check out Engstrom, Stackley, and Brunt, the law firm that's representing Schmidt."

Donna and Roman listened without speaking.

"I want to find out what they're up to and which of their people will be involved with the Schmidt case. Also they represent the Omniglade Foundation, which is being audited by the IRS. See what's going on with that.

Donna and Roman nodded.

CHAPTER 4

CONTINUING LEGAL EDUCATION

"How did I get roped into this?" Donna protested as Brenda, the woman from the FBI's technical support unit, secured the small transmitting device under the waistband of Donna's skirt. Attached to the transmitter was a thin wire that ended in a decorative cloverleaf pin. Brenda led the wire delicately under Donna's blouse from the transmitter to a spot just below Donna's left shoulder and attached it to the blouse. The pin was a tiny but sensitive microphone that picked up nearby sounds and transmitted them by radio waves to a receiving device.

"I'm not a cop," Donna grumbled, "and I'm certainly not an actor."

"You'll do great," Roman assured Donna from a discreet distance. "You're a natural."

"I'm not sure what I'm a natural at, but this definitely is not it."

"Look, Donna, we've got a short window of opportunity and you're all we've got at the moment. Hannigan and Klein are on board with this."

"Did the judge OK the search warrant?"

"Klein ran it over to the judge's chambers personally and got it signed off."

Donna tucked the blouse into the waist of her skirt and shifted slightly, trying to get comfortable with the device. It still didn't feel right.

"Shit. I'm going to screw this up."

"Stop thinking about it; just relax and remember that you're going in as your friend Lori De Luca." Roman helped her with the matching suit jacket. "C'mon. We've got to get going. It's almost three."

"Let me see his picture again," Donna said, picking up her slim attaché case.

Roman showed her the picture of Dennis Brunt as they walked out the door to the elevator.

"This could be a violation of the attorney-client privilege," Donna went on.

"Don't steer the discussion to the Schmidt case," Roman reminded Donna, "but if Brunt does blurt out something about Schmidt, Klein will decide if he wants to use it."

They parted company in the street. Donna walked from the Dirksen building to the Chicago Bar Association building on Plymouth Court and took the elevator to the fourth floor. After checking in at the registration desk, she picked up the written material for the Continuing Legal Education course on entertainment law and peered into the conference room. It was a simple, rectangular-shaped room with a row of perhaps thirty or forty chairs facing a podium with a microphone. She spotted Brunt sitting by himself about halfway back from the podium. Several chairs on either side of him were empty. She could easily pick a seat close to him, but she hesitated—it might seem too aggressive, she thought.

Donna considered waiting for the room to fill up more so that choosing a seat close to him wouldn't seem so obvious. She glanced back at the entrance. People were entering in a steady stream and the room was starting to fill up. If she waited too long someone could take the seats next to Brunt.

Screw the social norms, she said to herself, *you're a big girl now.*

She walked over to Brunt and plopped herself down with a flourish in the seat next to his.

"Is this seat taken?" she asked, looking at him with as much of a friendly attitude as she could muster. This was way past her comfort zone.

Dennis glanced back at her. "No. Sit down, please," he said. His tone and body language felt friendly rather than perfunctory, Donna thought. He didn't seem to pick up on her nervousness—at least he was enough of a gentleman to not let on.

"Thank you. I'm Lori De Luca," Donna said, extending her hand. Her smile got a little easier.

"Hi. I'm Dennis Brunt," he said, taking her hand lightly. He noticed that she wasn't wearing a ring.

There was a moment of silence as Donna made an effort to settle into her seat. She took out some note paper from her attaché case with a little more flourish than was necessary.

"I take it your practice is in entertainment law?" Dennis ventured.

"No. I'm in general practice," Donna answered, relieved that Dennis made an effort to maintain the friendly chatter. "I thought about getting into it, though. How about you?"

"I'm a tax lawyer," he said, "but I'm looking too."

Donna crossed her right leg over the left one and leaned toward him slightly. Her eyes gazed politely in Dennis's direction.

"I signed up for the course on a lark," Dennis went on. "I wanted to get involved in something other than the technical tax stuff I usually deal with."

Donna started to relax a little more and her smile became easier.

"I noticed that this course deals with film production in Chicago," Dennis continued. "It's a nice change of pace. Plus I like the movie connection."

They chatted before the course started, and then again briefly during the break when they went to the back of the conference room and nibbled on some of the snacks and soft drinks laid out on a table. They seemed to be hitting it off, Donna thought. Dennis invited her for a drink after the course ended at six that evening and Donna accepted. They shared a cab to a restaurant in Greektown. Roman Kaminski and another FBI agent followed them at a safe distance in an unmarked car. Roman monitored and recorded the conversation from the wire Donna was wearing while the other agent drove.

Donna and Dennis sat down by the bar and ordered drinks. Donna asked Dennis what attracted him to entertainment law.

"I like movies," he said, "old movies."

"Me too," she said, holding off from any further expansion. She wanted to see how much encouragement he needed to go on.

"I just saw *The African Queen* again recently on the TCM channel," Dennis went on, "with Humphrey Bogart and Katharine Hepburn."

"Yeah, I saw it too," Donna smiled easily. This surreptitious stuff wasn't as tough as she had feared. "It won an Academy Award, didn't it?"

"Bogart won it for best actor; the only one he ever won, actually."

Donna began to chat a little easier. She told Dennis that she liked the dancing musicals with Fred Astaire and Ginger Rogers.

"Me too," Dennis said. "Fred Astaire was an incredible dancer."

"So was Ginger Rogers," Donna smiled. "She did everything he did except in high heels and backwards."

"Didn't Ann Richards say that," Dennis smiled back, "the Governor of Texas?"

"Yes she did, at the Democratic National Convention in 1988. But I liked the line so much I checked it out. It's supposed to have originated with a Frank and Ernest cartoon in 1982."

Dennis invited Donna for dinner. They moved over to the dining area and Donna excused herself to go to the powder room. She checked to make sure the booths were unoccupied and then got into one.

"I feel like a creep," she spoke in a hushed tone into the pin on her lapel. "He seems like a nice guy. I'm not getting any relevant information from him. I'm going to turn this thing off."

"You're doing great," Roman encouraged her. "See if you can get him to talk about the Schmidt case."

"I thought I wasn't supposed to steer the conversation to Schmidt."

"Let's see what we get out of this. Klein can decide what he wants to use."

"Screw it. I don't want to do this anymore," Donna hissed.

"Keep it down!" Roman pushed back. "You've got his confidence. Encourage him to have a few more drinks."

Another woman came into the bathroom and Donna stopped. She flushed the toilet and walked out after a perfunctory handwashing.

"Anything good on the menu?" Donna asked, rejoining Dennis in the dining area.

"Their lamb and seafood are good."

As they continued their conversation, Donna detached a part of herself to observe Dennis from an objective distance. He was about six feet tall and appeared to be generally in good shape, but not a body builder type. He was in his early thirties, she guessed, and had brown hair. His complexion was white, although it had a tinge of olive, perhaps from a Mediterranean or Latin American gene pool, she thought. He was low key and unassuming—certainly not pushy. That made it easier to carry on a conversation. She was grateful for that.

The waitress came over and took their orders.

"I'm going to Argentina in a few days," Dennis offered by way of conversation.

"That sounds wonderful," Donna commented brightly. "Is it business or personal?"

"It seems to be a combination of both."

"I'm sure there must be wonderful things to see and do. Are you traveling by yourself?"

"Some people from the law firm are going with me," Dennis went on, but stopped short. He didn't want to disclose too much due to the attorney-client privilege. He changed the subject abruptly.

"But tell me a little more about yourself, Lori. Are you going anywhere for the holidays?"

"I'm going to spend it with my parents," Donna said. She decided to reveal some true personal details about herself. She felt uncomfortable talking from the point of view of her assumed identity. If the conversation got more involved she might trip up or sound unsure about any details related to her friend Lori.

"My mom is a violinist," Donna went on, "so I might take in one of her concerts with my dad."

Donna wanted to be honest with him, but it was a delicate balance. She had a professional role to play.

"You didn't go into music, like your mother?" he asked.

"I took some violin lessons when I was little, but that didn't last very long. I think I inherited more of the genes from my dad's side."

The waitress brought their orders to the table: grilled salmon for him, stewed lamb for her. Dennis broke off a small portion of the grilled salmon with his fork and guided it carefully into his mouth.

"What does your dad do?" he asked.

"He's a financial analyst, but his dad, my grandfather, was a lawyer." Donna tackled the lamb.

"Well, I guess you found your niche," Dennis observed.

"I'm not sure about that. I'm thinking of switching fields, or getting out of law altogether. I think I have some recessive genes from my grandmother's side."

"Oh?" Dennis sensed that she was starting to open up. He wanted to encourage her. "What was she like?"

"She worked in the circus before my grandfather, the lawyer, married her and made a respectable woman out of her." Donna smiled, glancing at Dennis as she sipped her wine.

Dennis smiled back. He liked the story. "What did she do in the circus?" he asked.

"She was the pretty girl with the magician. She got sawed in half repeatedly and was miraculously pieced together every time."

"What about you?" Donna switched the focus back to Dennis. "You're not happy with law?"

"I don't know. I'm tired of transactional tax work. I thought I'd like it when I studied accounting in college. It seemed logical and predictably structured. Now I'm having second thoughts about it."

"Maybe you've got some recessive genes, too," Donna made a light effort to draw him out further.

Dennis didn't answer right away.

"I'm sorry," Donna caught herself, "your dad's a lawyer, isn't he?"

"I didn't say," Dennis responded, "but yes. My adoptive dad is a lawyer at our law firm. His name is Joseph Brunt."

Donna realized she had slipped up. Her knowledge about Dennis's father came from the briefing from Roman, not from what Dennis had said. The wine had loosened her up. She made a mental note to be more careful.

"I didn't know you had been adopted. My apologies, I didn't mean to pry."

"No apologies needed. I was adopted when I was five. I was born in Argentina."

"That's incredibly interesting. You're going to Argentina in a few days. Do you know who your natural parents are?

"I know who my mother is. I hope to see her."

Donna had stopped eating and was almost staring at Dennis.

"I never knew my father," Dennis went on. "Maybe I'll find out who he is—or was."

Donna checked herself. The conversation had become too personal. She was intrigued to know more, but decided she'd better let up. Her main job was to learn more about Schmidt, not Dennis.

"I would love to learn more about you, Dennis. I hope there will be another opportunity for us to chat."

"I would like that," Dennis said. They exchanged cell phone numbers.

CHAPTER 5

ARGENTINA

The Learjet landed at Ezeiza Airport, on the outskirts of Buenos Aires. It was nine in the evening locally, two hours later than Chicago time. The sun had already set, but it was still pleasantly warm. Dennis knew that the seasons in the southern hemisphere were reversed; it was the beginning of summer in Argentina.

He felt tired and grungy from the long flight—even after the layover in Caracas—and there still remained an hour's drive to downtown Buenos Aires. Two young men, both six footers, helped with the luggage and steered Dennis and Rico through customs. They loaded the luggage into the trunk of a stretch limo.

"This is a Mercedes-Benz S-Class Pullman," Rico commented, admiring their transportation. "An S-600 Pullman, to be exact," he added. "It has a twelve-cylinder engine that can generate three hundred sixty-seven horses, if pushed."

The two young men sat in the front while the passengers, including Dennis, Rico, Captain Arroyo, Mendoza the navigator, and Amanda, the pretty flight attendant, accommodated themselves in the back. There were two well-cushioned bench seats facing each other, with ample legroom between them. Dennis took the seat by the window, facing front; he never liked to travel looking backwards. Rico sat to his right. The flight crew sat opposite, with Amanda in the middle.

The limo was equipped with a TV monitor, a DVD, tape recorder, radio, separate earplugs, and a mini bar with a cooler. Dennis treated himself to a bottle of Evian mineral water from the cooler and stretched his legs.

There was little chatter among them. Some closed their eyes and began to doze; others put on earplugs and listened to music. The ride was soft and comfortable as they zipped along smartly on the General Ricchieri Expressway heading toward downtown Buenos Aires.

Dennis gazed out the window and absently noted the passing panorama. It was mostly countryside, a mixture of trees and fields with occasional houses or small commercial buildings scattered loosely, like seeds strewn carelessly by a farmer planting his spring crop. With half-closed eyes he noticed a large SUV in the adjoining lane. It pulled up alongside their limo and synchronized its speed. A man in the front right side of the SUV rolled down his window and started to gesture to the limo driver. The man spoke urgently, moving his left hand in a circular motion.

Dennis roused slightly from his lethargy. It appeared that the man was gesturing their limo driver to open the window. *Maybe he's lost or something*, Dennis thought to himself.

The limo driver glanced over to the man in the SUV and pushed the window button on the armrest of his door. As the window glided down, the man in the SUV raised his right hand and pointed it at the limo driver. It held a pistol. The pistol fired. The limo driver's head exploded into shards of bone, spurts of blood, and pieces of flesh. His body slumped over to the right and his hands dropped from the steering wheel. The limo veered sharply to the right and headed toward a ditch.

A flash went off in Dennis's head as a shot of adrenaline jolted him into heightened awareness. In what seemed like a slow-motion replay, Dennis observed with incredible sharpness the onrush of events. His right hand bolted out reflexively in an effort to shield himself from the certain apocalypse.

Amanda and Captain Arroyo, who had both been seated with their backs to the front, jerked up suddenly. "Oh my God!" Amanda shouted, her eyes ablaze.

Captain Arroyo raised his right hand and attempted to turn awkwardly toward the front in an effort to face the danger. Mendoza woke up with a startle and looked up in fear and confusion, unable to understand what was happening.

Rico let out a sharp yelp and lunged toward the front seat. He grabbed the driver's slumped body by the collar and jerked it over to the left. "Grab the wheel!" he shouted to the other young man in the front. "Grab the fucking wheel!"

The man, who had been frozen momentarily in fear and confusion, sprang to action. He shoved the dead driver's body to the left, grabbed control of the wheel and yanked it sharply to the left. The limo, which was still traveling at a good speed, veered back into the right lane of the expressway. It had been only inches away from careening into the ditch.

Rico, whose hands were now smeared with the driver's blood and flesh, yanked the body further to the left. "Get over to your left more," he ordered the young man. "See if you can get your foot on the brake."

The young man slid over to the left, pushing the bloodied body of the driver toward the door, trying to take control of the wheel.

The SUV, which was just ahead, braked sharply and slowed down in an apparent effort to align along the driver's side of the limo again. The man on the right side of the SUV pointed his pistol toward the limo again, waiting to get into position to take another shot.

"Put your head down!" Rico barked to the young man trying to steer the limo. "As low as you can." He yanked Mendoza away from the left back window and pushed him down onto the floor. "Get down every-body!" he shouted.

Dennis and the others hustled clumsily to get out of his way. Rico pulled out a Beretta from the chest holster inside his jacket, released the safety catches, and pushed the back window button on the door panel. A rush of air and whooshing noise filled the back.

Rico aimed the Beretta toward the SUV and fired off three shots. One put a hole in the right front door of the SUV, just below the window. The second one shattered the window on the driver's side. The third one found its mark. The face of the man with the pistol contorted into a death mask as he slumped sideways toward the driver.

The SUV's tires let out a screech as it accelerated away from the limo into the dark distance.

In spite of the young man's valiant effort to steer the limo, it slid into a ditch on the right side of the road and crashed into a sign. Fortunately, the ditch wasn't deep and he managed to steer the vehicle to a rough stop. It didn't roll over, but it tilted precariously to the right. The engine was still running, but the loose items inside the car—bottles of water, soda, liquor, drinking glasses, small pieces of luggage—were scattered all over the floor and seats.

Rico got out of the limo and the others followed. He examined the damage to the vehicle. It had sustained a sizable dent to the bumper and the fender on the right side and knocked out the light. It also appeared that the radiator was leaking fluid and the right tire was flat; the left side was OK. The left headlight was still on and cast an eerie shaft in the dark.

Rico opened the driver's side door and lowered the body to the ground. He checked for a pulse. "He's dead," Rico pronounced.

The young man who had steered the limo to a stop gave Rico a funny look. At first it looked as though he was going to smile. He let out a short laugh, almost like a bark. Then, slowly, his expression changed to one of sadness. He extended his right hand toward Rico, as though he wanted to ask him a question. But he didn't say anything. His eyes seemed unfocused. Then his face turned to the dead man on the ground. His eyes filled with tears. He lowered himself to his knees and covered his face with his hands. He stayed that way for a while. His hunched shoulders shuddered periodically, but there was no sound.

He then lowered his hands to his sides, fists clenched, and raised his head. He seemed to look to the sky. "*Hijo de puta!*" he screamed. "*Hijo de la gran puta!*"

Rico walked over slowly to the young man and rested his hand gently on his shoulder.

"You did a good job," Rico said to him. "You saved our lives."

"You don't understand," the young man said, looking up at Rico. "He is my brother. He is my *brother*," he shouted.

"I'm sorry," Rico said quietly. "I'm very sorry."

Dennis and the others moved instinctively into a semicircle around the kneeling man and his dead brother. They stood silently, like pallbearers, looking down at the ground, not knowing what to say. They grieved with him; they felt his grief.

But this wasn't a good time to grieve; the situation wasn't settled yet, it was still fraught with danger. Rico broke the silence. "We have to call for help immediately," he said, his voice slightly hoarse. "These people, whoever they are, may be back. Does anyone have a cellular phone that works here?"

"I do," Amanda said, moving toward the back door of the limo. "I'll call my dad. He'll get some help for us."

"We don't need your dad," Rico barked angrily. "We need the police."

"My dad is the US ambassador here," Amanda said calmly. "He'll get the police and the Marines, if need be."

She found her purse in the jumble of strewn items in the back of the limo and pulled out her cellular phone. She hit a button and they listened to the ringing; she must have had the speaker on. There was a click and a man answered.

"Hi Amanda," he said cheerily. "Are you back in town?"

"Dad!" Amanda spoke urgently. "There's been a terrible accident. Our driver was shot and is dead. We're afraid that they might be back again. Can you come and get us?"

"What? Where are you? Are you OK?" he shouted.

"I'm OK. We're about halfway back into town from Ezeiza. We're in a ditch alongside the road, in a stretch limo."

"I'll get a helicopter and fly out there immediately. We should be there in about fifteen or twenty minutes. Are the police there yet?"

"No. This just happened a few minutes ago. You're the first one we called."

"I'll have someone notify the police at once. In the meantime, is there any way you can protect yourselves?"

"One of the men here has a pistol. He shot one of the attackers."

"Good. Take cover, if you can. See if you can find some bushes or trees. Put the hazard blinkers on so that we can find you. And for God's sake, don't lose that phone."

"OK Dad," Amanda concluded. "Please hurry."

"Thanks, Amanda," Rico said. He hit the button on the dashboard for the hazard blinkers. The red lights started to blink in the darkness. Somehow they reminded Dennis of a broken neon hotel sign in the sleazy part of town. *How stupid is that?* Dennis thought.

"Keep the motor running," Rico added. "And leave the lights on, at least the one that still works. That'll help them to spot us. In the meantime, I need some help with the luggage."

He unlocked the trunk and the others helped him take out some of the bags.

"This one," he said, pointing to a particular piece of luggage. "Open it, please."

Rico placed his hands in the suitcase and took out three pistols.

"Does anybody know how to use these?" he asked.

Captain Arroyo and Mendoza stepped forward. Rico armed the pistols with cartridges and instructed them about the safety catches.

"If these people come back before help arrives, we want to be ready for them," Rico said.

"How about the third one?" he asked, looking around.

Dennis hesitated. He wondered how Rico had got the pistols past security at the airport in Chicago.

"I'll take it," the young driver said, standing up. He looked to be back in control of himself. "I know how to use pistols."

"What's your name?" Rico asked, handing him the last pistol.

"Armando," he said. "Armando Montero. I hope those fucking bastards come back. I want to get a shot at them."

"You did a good job, Armando," Rico said again. "You saved our lives."

I better learn how to use those things, Dennis thought to himself.

CHAPTER 6

ESTANCIA EL REPOSO

Arturo Sandoval had a full head of black hair that was combed straight back. It didn't look flat though, there was so much of it. It dominated his face, a mixture of regular Hispanic features and a hint of native Indian blended in, just enough to exclude him from the upper reaches of the white Spanish settlers that had first colonized Argentina over four hundred and fifty years ago.

When you first met him you had the sense that he knew exactly who he was and where he fit into the fabric of society. He didn't speak much—but then, he didn't have to. His six-foot-two 220-pound frame, coupled with his calm and logical manner, established his presence naturally—in most situations.

That combination was what first brought him to Gerhard Schmidt's attention. Schmidt had hired him ten years previously as his personal bodyguard, luring him out of the military where Sandoval had distinguished himself as a marksman and a munitions specialist in his three years of service. Schmidt assigned him to Dennis Brunt and Rico Monzoni after the shooting incident from the airport.

Sandoval sat behind the wheel of the Land Rover for the two-and-a-half-hour drive from Buenos Aires to Estancia El Reposo. Alejandro Montoya, the other bodyguard, sat next to him. He was younger than Sandoval, and smaller—about five foot ten and 170 pounds—but you got the sense that he was lightning quick and tough, bordering on mean. He was a true mestizo, a full mixture of Spanish and Indian. He had played on a professional soccer team in Argentina before the ACL on his right knee snapped and he was sidelined for a year. He never went back after that.

They both carried pistols and several rifles that were stored under the front seat of the Land Rover, with additional arms and ammunition in the trunk. They spoke little throughout the trip, only when spoken to.

Dennis and Rico sat in the back seat. They settled in for the long drive through the countryside and chatted from time to time. Dennis still felt unsettled by the violent incident on the highway the day before.

"We owe you a debt of gratitude," Dennis said, turning to Rico. "If it hadn't been for your fast thinking and your gun, we could have all been killed."

"I like to carry a pistol with me at all times," Rico said. "For protection."

"I can certainly see why you need protection here in Argentina," Dennis observed.

"Buenos Aires can be a dangerous place," Rico mused. "Once you get past the veneer of tourism, there's a very real world beneath the surface."

"I guess I led a sheltered life till now," Dennis observed. "Unless you live in the projects on the South Side of Chicago, life isn't that dramatic."

"I'm not sure about that," Rico answered. "Sometimes you run across rough characters in Chicago, even outside the projects."

Dennis remained silent, not sure of what to say.

"You know I do investigative work for the law firm, don't you?" Rico glanced at Dennis.

"Yeah, I know," Dennis answered, somewhat tentatively.

"What do you think criminal defense work involves, investment counseling?"

"No, it doesn't. I guess I just hadn't gotten involved in that aspect of it."

Rico paused for a while. "I think you will with this Schmidt case," he said.

"By the way," Dennis asked, "how did you get those pistols past security at the airport in Chicago?"

"I came on the plane with a flight crew badge. They don't check the flight crew, or the luggage they carry, especially on a private flight."

Dennis nodded. He was curious about the whole concept of gun ownership. He had never owned or used them before, although he knew that some people were passionate about them.

"I guess you own a few guns," Dennis smiled at Rico, attempting to broaden the conversation.

"I inherited my father's passion for guns," Rico said picking up the cue. "I grew up seeing them and hearing him talk about them. So I guess it's in my genes."

Rico pulled out a pistol from inside his jacket, the one he had used to ward off the attackers, and laid it flat in the palm of his right hand.

"It's a Beretta, a ninety-six Brigadier," Rico explained. "The ninety-six is a forty-caliber version of the ninety-two, which is used by the US military, except the ninety-two is known as the M9 in the military."

Dennis listened attentively. His interest wasn't so much a fascination with guns per se as with the proximity of a lethal weapon.

"Beretta is an Italian manufacturer that has a history going back to the early sixteenth century," Rico went on. "It was started by Mastro Bartolomeo Beretta."

Dennis nodded.

"The family continues to run it today," Rico continued. "In fact, they have a store here in Buenos Aires, which they call a gallery. It's close to the Plaza Vicente Lopez, if you're familiar with Buenos Aires."

"I left Buenos Aires when I was five, so I don't remember much. How does the gun work?" Dennis ventured to ask.

"It is a semiautomatic, which means that the chamber is loaded automatically after each firing; you don't have to reload it manually. All you have to do is press the trigger again to fire the next round."

"If this is a *semi*automatic," Dennis asked, "what is an *auto*matic?"

"A fully automatic pistol or rifle will continue to fire for as long as you hold the trigger depressed, until the magazine is empty."

Dennis observed silently.

"The bullets are held in the magazine," Rico continued. He pressed the magazine release button at the bottom of the pistol grip and pulled it out. He then pushed it back in and clicked it locked.

"You can fire off ten rounds in a matter of seconds—eleven if you have an extra round in the chamber."

Dennis was drawn in by the matter-of-fact, almost mathematical tone Rico assumed in discussing the workings of the gun. It was a dispassionate discussion of a very dangerous thing, somewhat like a masked and gowned surgeon discussing the removal of a kidney from the body of an anesthetized patient on the operating table. All that was missing was the large, circular lamp overhead, the one that cast no shadows.

"Would you like to hold it?" Rico asked, extending his hand slightly in Dennis's direction. "It's OK," Rico added, "all the safety locks are on."

Dennis reached for the gun and curled his fingers carefully around the grip. The design naturally led the index finger toward the trigger mechanism, but Dennis placed the tip of it carefully on the front of the trigger guard.

"Your instincts are good," Rico commented. "You're handling it like a pro."

The weight of the gun felt comfortable; about two and a half pounds, he guessed.

"Why don't you hold on to it," Rico said. "I'll set up some target practice for us at a gun club here in Buenos Aires so you learn how to use it."

Dennis hesitated. "I'm not licensed to use it."

"We'll take care of it," Rico assured him.

● ● ●

The tires of the Land Rover crunched on the gravel of the long driveway as Sandoval steered the vehicle toward the main building of Estancia El Reposo. It was about eleven o'clock Sunday morning and there was little visible movement. Sandoval parked in front of the entrance and popped the trunk open. Montoya started to unload the few bags of luggage. Dennis got out of the vehicle and stretched while Rico rubbed his eyes.

There was a rustic feel to the place; you could tell you were in the country. The air was fresh and clean, although traces of newly cut grass and a mild aroma of horse manure wafted with the light breezes. It was a sunny morning, with the temperature in the mid-seventies, Dennis surmised, though he expected that it would probably rise into the eighties by mid-afternoon. Several birds chattered periodically and fluttered about from branch to branch, engaged in some playful dance ritual.

The main building, though obviously old, had a strong, two-story façade dominated by the stone stairway leading up to the entrance, which was recessed into a private patio.

The door in the recess cracked open and Dennis heard muffled voices and the scurrying of feet. In a minute the door swung fully open and a woman, probably in her mid-thirties, started to descend the stairs. She was accompanied by a man and a woman who followed several steps behind. Dennis and the others stopped what they were doing and turned to look at her. She was stunningly beautiful.

"Hello," she said, extending her hand toward Dennis as she reached the bottom of the stairs. "My name is Esmeralda Atoche." She looked straight into Dennis's eyes. Her manner was professional, but friendly and open. There was no trace of arrogance or diva ego, though she could easily have been an actress or a model. She probably had been one, or both, Dennis thought.

"Hello," Dennis managed to say without stammering. He was mesmerized by her green eyes and the lips that were curved into an easy smile.

"Welcome to Estancia El Reposo," she continued, taking back her hand. Dennis had forgotten to let go of it.

"I want you to meet Hector Torres," she said, turning to the man alongside of her. "He is the general manager here."

Dennis shook hands with Torres, a muscular man of about forty. Torres didn't say anything, or even smile. Dennis sensed aggressiveness from Torres, bordering on animosity. Maybe it was the instant jealousy a man feels when he sees a potential rival to a beautiful woman, but Dennis suspected that there was something more. At any rate, Torres managed to snap Dennis out of his infatuation mode.

"This is Enrico Monzoni," Dennis said, turning to Rico, who took turns shaking hands with Esmeralda and Torres.

"Danguole is in charge of the accommodations here," Esmeralda continued, turning toward the middle-aged woman standing behind her. "She will show you to your rooms."

Dennis and Rico turned to follow Danguole, trailed by Sandoval and Montoya with the luggage.

"Oh, and one more thing," Esmeralda added. "We will be having lunch at one o'clock in the main dining room. Please join us."

Dennis and Rico nodded. Danguole took them to their accommodation, which was basically a large room with two windows facing east. The windows had wooden shutters that could be closed—probably for the afternoon siesta, Dennis thought. Their beds were next to each other. Dennis thought he would be comfortable, but wondered whether Rico's huge frame would fit. He asked Danguole whether she could get a larger one for Rico.

"I'll see what I can do," she answered, giving Dennis a slight curtsey.

"Thank you, Danguole," Dennis answered. He sensed that she was sincere and he could trust her.

"By the way," he added, "what kind of name is Danguole?"

"It's Lithuanian," she said, smiling back at Dennis. "Most people think it's too hard to pronounce, though, so you can call me Dange."

"OK, Dange," Dennis smiled back. "Thank you."

Dennis started to unpack his handbag. It was quiet there, country quiet, and he began to feel a little more relaxed. He looked at Rico, who had flopped down on the bed and lit up a cigarette.

"You know," Dennis spoke first, "I'm just curious. Is it me or is everybody treating me like I'm Prince Philip?"

Rico smiled and took another puff.

"Well," he said, "you *are* an emissary of Schmidt. He owns all this stuff."

"Yeah, I guess you're right," Dennis said, hanging up one of his shirts in the dresser. "I just sense that there's something more."

"We also got shot at and made the news," Rico noted. "That makes us celebrities of sorts."

"Maybe I'm making too much of it," Dennis concluded. "But I can't say that I'm used to all this attention. It makes me uneasy."

Two young men walked in through the open door and asked Rico if they could take the bed. They said they would bring him a larger one. Rico stood up and positioned himself by the door. He watched as the workmen disassembled the bed and began to carry away the pieces.

Dennis remembered that he'd had several calls while he had slept in Buenos Aires, including one from Linda. There was no telephone in the room, so he got hold of one of Schmidt's Globalstar satellite phones that Sandoval picked up in Buenos Aires. Rico had taken a great deal of interest in it on the ride over to the estancia. He said it was capable of reaching virtually any phone in the world from even the remotest regions by beaming up to any of the forty-eight low-Earth orbit satellites that happened to be overhead at that time and place.

Dennis dialed Linda's home phone number.

"Hello?" the voice answered with a lilt toward a question mark. It was Linda's.

"Hi," Dennis said lightly. "It's me."

"Dennis!" Linda's voice jumped an octave into the upper register. "Are you OK?"

"Yeah, I'm OK. Rico is too." His voice was low key and relaxed. He wanted to reassure Linda that everything was fine.

"I was worried when I heard what happened," she said.

"Yeah, it was pretty tense for a while," he said, standing up from his bed. The two young men were bringing in the frame of the larger bed and he wanted to give them room. They had to tilt it sideways to get it through the door. Rico observed the operation from the far end of the room.

"Is it safe to be there?" Linda asked.

"We've got a couple of Schmidt's personal bodyguards now. They look like they know what they're doing. We'll be OK. How are you doing?"

"I'm OK."

"Anything going on in Chicago?"

"Kevin's debate with Clayton has been scheduled for mid-January. It's going to be televised."

"That's sounds good. A televised debate with the incumbent usually favors the challenger, doesn't it?"

"Yeah, it usually does. But there are rumors that he's going to make negative allegations against Kevin."

"What kind of negative allegations?"

"For improper campaign contributions."

Dennis watched the young men bring in the box springs and the mattress through the open door. Rico lit up another cigarette.

"Does Kevin have anything to worry about?" Dennis asked.

"I don't know," Linda said.

"Where are the improper contributions supposedly coming from?"

"The Omniglade Foundation."

Dennis fell silent momentarily. He wasn't sure how to react to that. "Is there any truth to those allegations?" he asked.

"I don't think so," Linda said. "But I don't really know. I don't get involved in the financial end of it."

"Who does?"

"Stackley. And Kevin, I suppose."

Dennis was silent again. He looked over to Dange, who had just walked in the door to supervise the making of Rico's bed. She looked at Dennis. Next to her stood a woman in her fifties.

It was his mother.

The satellite phone dropped from Dennis's hand on to the hardwood floor with a bang. A plastic piece broke off and bounced with a clatter to the base of the dresser.

CHAPTER 7

REUNION

She had aged considerably. When he left that morning twenty-eight years ago she was in her early to mid-twenties, at most. Now she was a mature woman in her early fifties, though you could still see traces of the beauty that attracted men.

She stood in the doorway, afraid of how Dennis would react, not daring to approach him. Her hands were clasped together in front of her, almost like a prayer gesture. Her eyes were ablaze with alertness and happiness, but also with sadness and regret. Tears welled up in them as she looked with entreaty at Dennis.

"Dennis," her lips whispered his name in her native Spanish pronunciation, "*mi querido* Dennis."

Rico picked up the satellite phone from the floor and told Linda that Dennis would call her back. He then walked out of the room with Dange, who gestured for the two workers to follow.

Dennis was conflicted about approaching his mother. On the one hand, she was his mother; on the other, she was this strange woman. He had these strong emotional memories of her from childhood, but then she was also a woman he didn't know or understand. All those years he had been angry about having been given up for adoption. He felt he had been abandoned without explanation, without ever hearing from his mother again.

"I don't know what to say." Dennis finally spoke up, looking at her. He didn't want to show the anger and confusion he had felt all those years. That would have been impolite and would have precluded any sort of meaningful communication. Worst of all, it would have hurt this woman who looked so frail and helpless. "I hope we'll be able to talk and reestablish the bond that was broken," he ventured to say.

"Yes, *querido* Dennis," she said, tears running down her cheeks. "I would like that very much."

There were several chairs in the room. He pulled one closer and asked her to sit down.

"Can I get you something to drink?" he asked.

"No, thank you," she answered. "I just want to sit near you and talk to you. I want to take your hand and kiss it, and ask for your forgiveness." More tears ran down her cheeks.

Dennis felt embarrassed but moved by this simple, almost childish declaration. He reached out and took her hand in his.

"Please don't kiss it," he said, trying to control his emotions. "And please don't cry."

She was silent, her eyes downcast.

"I guess I just need to understand what happened," he continued, squeezing her hand. He was embarrassed to look at her because his eyes were starting to tear up.

"Yes, I want to explain everything," she said, brushing away the tears from her cheeks with her free hand. Dennis took a tissue from the dispenser on the nightstand and dabbed her cheeks with it.

"I don't know if this is a good time to talk about things like this," she said, taking some fresh tissues from the dispenser and blowing her nose with them. The nearby wastebasket started to fill up rapidly.

"I did not want you to be raised here," she said by way of a tentative explanation. "I did not want you to become like your older brother."

Dennis remembered his brother, Marko. He had adored him when he was growing up. Marko was his role model and Dennis followed him whenever Marko would let him.

"I didn't know that Marko was a problem," Dennis said, surprised at his mother's comment.

"He was starting to be with the wrong crowd, with kids that were a bad influence on him," his mother said, looking down at her hands, which were folded on her lap. "I did not want you to fall into the same crowd."

"Couldn't we have moved?" Dennis asked. "Wouldn't it have been easier than sending me away?"

"I thought about that," she said, "but it was not possible."

"Why not?"

"That crowd was made up of the children of the friends and associates of his father, and yours. He would not allow us to move, to break away from it."

Dennis stood up from his chair and walked to one of the windows. He looked through the shutters into the patio and garden in the back of the house. A stone wall, bleached white, was visible in the distance.

"That's another thing," he said. "I never knew who my father was."

There was a silence that lasted maybe ten seconds. Dennis finally turned to look at his mother, waiting for her to speak. Her head was down and tears were falling onto the tissue she held in her hands. She twisted and turned the tissue until it was shredded into small pieces. But she didn't dab her eyes with it, she was too distracted for that.

"Marko's father and yours," she said, "is Gerhard Schmidt."

Dennis felt a thud in his chest, as if someone had landed a punch. He couldn't breathe momentarily and put his hand against the wall for support.

He'd had vague premonitions about that, but he'd pushed them away. Now he realized that he'd pushed them away, probably unconsciously, because they were too scary to deal with.

"But why...?" Dennis began to utter some words, but they came out in disjointed fragments. "Why would you...?"

His mother stood up and walked over to Dennis by the window. She stood close to him but didn't touch him. Dennis faced the wall, head bowed. His right hand was raised above his head, resting against the wall for support.

"Why would I get involved with a man like that?" his mother finished his sentence. "Because I was young when I first met him—fifteen—and beautiful, and came from a very poor family. He was handsome and rich and exciting to be with. He offered me a chance to break away from poverty."

Dennis listened silently to her, still facing the wall.

"I will not blame you if you judge me," his mother continued. "And I will not defend myself against any accusations that you would make—because they would be true."

Dennis turned slightly and mustered enough courage to glance at his mother's eyes. They were red from crying and welled up again. She looked up at Dennis and spotted the silver medallion of St. Christopher hanging around his neck. She reached up and touched it. She then cast her eyes down again.

"Oh, Dennis, my loved one," she spoke softly. "Do you know what poverty is? Do you know how dehumanizing it is?"

Dennis gazed out the window again into the garden. He could see the birds fluttering among the branches.

"I take it that he never married you," Dennis said. It was more of a statement than a question.

"No. We never married. He never even acknowledged paternity for you and Marko."

Dennis fell silent again. Her words hurt.

"But he always supported us," she went on, "and still does—provided we play by his rules."

There was a knock on the door. Dange opened it slightly and peered in.

"I'm sorry to interrupt," she said, "but I wanted to let you know that lunch will be served in a few minutes. Ms. Atoche asked that you join her in the dining room."

"Thank you, Dange," Dennis spoke, stirring from the stupor he felt. "We'll be there shortly."

He turned back to his mother. "But after you sent me away," he said, looking at her, "why didn't you call me, or write me? I wanted so much to hear from you."

His mother started to knead fresh pieces of tissue again.

"I wanted, with every part of my being, to see you, to hold you, to talk to you. But I could not. Once Gerhard agreed to let you go to America, he made it a condition that I was never to see you or speak to you again."

"But why would he do that? What possible reason could he have for being so cruel?"

"I don't know. Maybe it was his way of punishing me for wanting to take you away from his way of life, from his control."

Dennis let that thought sink in. He made a mental note to follow up on that with Schmidt.

"What about Marko?" Dennis asked. "Where is he?"

"He's here," she said. Dennis waited for her to continue, but she didn't. Her eyes were downcast again.

"Can I see him?"

"It's up to him. He knows you are here." Dennis sensed the brevity of her answers, the tension in his mother's voice.

"Is he OK?"

Her eyes welled up with tears again. "As he got older, he changed, especially after you left," she went on. "He never finished high school. He got into trouble with the police. He started drinking and taking drugs."

Dennis looked sadly at his mother. He wanted to reach out to her, to understand, to help, but he didn't know how.

"I tried as best I could, Dennis. He is my son, as are you. A mother's love never dies. I never gave up on him. I prayed to the Virgin Mary a thousand times. I tried everything I knew how."

"I'm so sorry," Dennis said. "I thought about him and about you every day and every night. Those feelings never left me."

They sat silently for several minutes. Words couldn't fill the void they both felt.

"C'mon," Dennis said finally, taking his mother's arm. "Let's go find Rico and get some lunch."

CHAPTER 8

FIESTA AT ESTANCIA EL REPOSO

Dennis and his mother, Aurelia, joined Rico, Sandoval, and Montoya in the lobby. They followed Dange through the hallway into the dining room. It was large and spacious, with a high ceiling and stained rafters. Heavy drapes, extending from the ceiling to the floor, were partly drawn. While some light from outdoors entered the room, there was a dark and somber feel to it, almost medieval. It helped to keep the room cool, Dennis surmised.

A long table, set in the middle, dominated the room. A number of people were already seated. Esmeralda was at the head of the table with Hector Torres, the general manager of the estancia, to her right.

Esmeralda looked gorgeous. Her black hair was pulled straight back in the traditional Spanish bun, held in place with an amber comb. Her alabaster skin, tinged with a hint of olive, curved smoothly over the high cheekbones and descended gracefully to her full red lips. Dennis's eyes continued on down to the oval of her chin, through her bare arms, and rested finally on her long and slender hands that were placed delicately on the end of the table.

Dange directed Dennis to sit to Esmeralda's left, with Rico one seat over. Dange sat at the foot of the table, opposite Esmeralda, and directed Dennis's mother to sit next to Rico. Dennis interrupted this formal choreography and motioned for his mother to sit next to him, between him and Rico. Torres stiffened visibly at this gesture, though Esmeralda nodded to Dange and smiled at Dennis.

"I want you to know, Dennis," Esmeralda said, "that we are happy to see you and that you are most welcome here."

"Thank you," Dennis said, pulling out a chair for his mother. "Rico and I appreciate your hospitality."

"I understand, Mr. Monzoni, that you have family here in Buenos Aires," Esmeralda said, turning to Rico.

"Yes. My parents live here. I hope to see them soon."

"I hear that your quick action and bravery Friday evening was responsible for saving the lives of Mr. Brunt and the other passengers in the limousine."

"Thank you. Although Enrique Montero wasn't so lucky."

"Yes. It was most unfortunate. Enrique was one of our best employees and the father of a baby girl. We have made the funeral arrangements."

Several young country girls brought in bowls of soup and placed them before the diners, starting with Esmeralda and Torres. It appeared to be a hearty chicken vegetable soup and looked delicious. Dennis was anxious to dig in, but waited until everyone was served.

"Has any progress been made on finding out who was responsible for the shooting?" Dennis asked, turning to Esmeralda.

"Not yet," she answered, placing a cloth napkin on her lap. "But Hector here is working with the police," she added, looking at Torres.

Hector Torres was forty years old and stood about five foot eight, Dennis surmised. He was wiry and muscular, handsome in a rugged way. His olive skin was leathery from constant exposure to the elements and was covered by a short beard and moustache.

He never married, Dennis found out later from his mother, and had a reputation for being a playboy and a ladies' man. A local boy, he grew up in the area and was hired by Schmidt's estancia as a *resero*, a cowboy, when he was still in his teens. Through skill in horsemanship and hard work, as well as natural leadership abilities, he worked his way up to a *dormador*, a horse tamer; to *capatáz*, a farm manager; and finally to an *estanciador*, a steward in charge of administrating the estancia.

"The police have a team of investigators working on this," Torres commented, placing a napkin on his lap.

Dennis tasted the soup after Esmeralda and everyone else had begun to eat. It tasted homemade. Dange informed them that the vegetables were from the garden in the estancia and the chicken had been boiled only several hours before.

"Have any private sources been contacted?" Dennis asked, turning to Torres.

Torres appeared startled by Dennis's question.

"I don't know what you mean by 'private sources,'" he said, furrowing his brow. "This is a police matter. I'm sure they are doing everything they can to get to the bottom of this."

"Well, I mean Schmidt isn't being investigated in Chicago for violating the Boy Scout oath," Dennis persisted. "I would think that he has some private contacts in the streets of Buenos Aires."

"Yes," Esmeralda interjected, surprised at Dennis's candor. "Gerhard instructed me to give you full access to all his files. Perhaps you and Mr. Monzoni will help us uncover some of those private contacts."

Esmeralda's comments seemed to be an effort to allay the tension that was starting to build up between Dennis and Torres.

"I would be careful if I were you, Mr. Brunt," Torres commented, sipping his soup. "You may be getting in over your head."

"I think I already am," Dennis responded dryly. His mother was visibly nervous. Her eyes were downcast as she sipped her soup quietly.

Dennis glanced toward the open door; Sandoval and Montoya were standing on either side of it. They became more alert at his glance. Raising a spoon to his mouth, Rico nodded slightly to Dennis.

Just then a man and a woman walked in noisily. The man had his arm around the woman's waist and they were both laughing at some private joke they had just shared.

Dennis stiffened visibly. The man was his brother Marko. He had a Fu Manchu mustache, and a slightly receding hairline, but otherwise it was unmistakably his brother. The woman was young, in her late teens, maybe, with bleached blond hair and a sensually languid body. They headed toward Hector Torres, who called for the servants to bring several more chairs to be placed next to him.

"Marko!" Esmeralda admonished him. "Aren't you going to say hello to your brother?"

"Hello, brother," Marko blurted out, trying to sound funny, although it didn't come out that way. His eyes were ablaze with the attempted humor, but the vulnerability was clearly visible. He sat down next to Torres.

Dennis stood up and walked toward Marko.

"Hello, Marko," Dennis offered his hand. "It's been a long time."

Marko reciprocated by extending his own hand to Dennis, although he remained seated, unsure of what to say. Dennis came closer to Marko and pulled gently on his hand, encouraging Marko to stand. Marko hesitated, but stood up. Dennis put his arm around Marko's shoulder and embraced him.

"You're my long-lost brother," Dennis said, "and I missed you very much."

Marko lost some of his attempted bravado and seemed genuinely affected by the embrace.

"So much time has gone by," Dennis went on, "time we can never recover. But maybe we can chat later, and try to reconnect."

Marko nodded, but didn't speak. Everyone in the room was silent.

"I will escort you personally, Dennis, to our headquarters in Buenos Aires," Esmeralda picked up where she had left off. "I understand that you are preparing a defense for Gerhard in the event that he is indicted."

"Yes," Dennis answered, walking back to his chair. "I will need to examine all the files and talk to everyone involved, even the clerks."

"I understand," Esmeralda nodded.

After lunch, everyone walked over to a large field behind the main building. Esmeralda explained that there would be displays of horsemanship by the gauchos who worked there, as well as several races. Dennis, his mother, and Rico settled into easy chairs in the shade of nearby trees; Esmeralda walked about helping to organize the events and attending to other matters that needed her attention. Torres busied himself with the gauchos, who were getting ready to put on a riding exhibition.

There was a festive atmosphere in the air. Several *payadors* circulated among the guests, playing their guitars in an effort to outwit each other with poetic contretemps. Rico explained that this was known as "the duel of the payadors, a form of entertainment for the guests."

Several calabash gourds of *mate*, a herbal tea, were passed around among the guests, who took sips through the elaborately etched silver straws called *bombillas*. Dennis took a sip of the mate, but found it quite bitter.

Rico smiled. "It's an acquired taste."

"What do you make of this guy Torres?" Dennis asked Rico.

"I don't trust him," Rico answered, sipping his mate.

"What about his relationship with Esmeralda?" Dennis asked, turning to his mother.

"He's in love with her," Aurelia stated flatly.

"Him and everybody else," Dennis replied.

"Does she reciprocate his affection?" Rico asked.

"Somewhat," Aurelia replied. "She knows how to keep a man interested without fully committing to him."

"What about her relationship with Schmidt?" Dennis asked.

"She became his lover about fifteen years ago," Aurelia answered, "shortly after Gerhard lost interest in me. They never married and he has had relationships with several other women during that time."

"But apparently he trusts her enough to let her run his operation here," Rico observed.

"It seems so," Aurelia said. "She's probably the closest thing he's ever had to a true wife. She knows enough not to push him into an exclusive relationship and he appreciates that."

Dennis, Rico, and Aurelia turned their attention to the workers, who were securing a wood board between two trees on either end of the field, about ten feet above the ground. Two rings were suspended from the board about six feet apart. Aurelia explained that this was being done in preparation for the Corrida De Sortijas, "Race of Rings," in which two riders would gallop simultaneously at full speed under the board and try to take the rings by inserting a little stick through them. The most skilled riders would receive prizes and the appreciation of the spectators.

A number of gauchos had already begun to gather with their horses and pranced about edgily in anticipation of the race. The undisputed champion of this event had been Hector Torres, but he retired from competition once he became the general manager of the estancia. The official explanation for his retirement was that it would not be fitting for the estanciador to be competing with the wash-and-tumble gauchos, but some of the gauchos mumbled to themselves that Torres had lost his edge. Of course, they wouldn't have had the nerve to say that to his face—unless they were drunk.

Torres stepped up to the field to preside over the race. He gave a signal for the race to begin and the first two riders galloped at full speed toward the rings. One of them succeeded in threading his ring through the stick.

"*Viva! Viva!*" The spectators rose to their feet and shouted with appreciation.

Two other gauchos lined up eagerly for their turn to race. One of them had a huge grin, but he was so drunk he almost fell off his horse.

"What about Torres's relationship to Gerhardt?" Dennis asked, turning to his mom. "He seems to be high up in the hierarchy."

"He's just behind Esmeralda," she answered. "His main function is to run the estancia, but he has begun to get involved in some of Gerhardt's other operations."

"What other operations?" Dennis asked.

"I'm not sure. He never shares those details with me. But since Gerhardt's troubles in Chicago, Torres has been more assertive."

"In what way?" Dennis asked.

"In just the way he walks and talks," Aurelia answered. "He seems to have more confidence now."

They watched as Torres raised his right arm high in the air and swung it down sharply, with the white handkerchief fluttering in his hand. Two more horsemen leaped forward into a full gallop, heading toward the suspended rings. One of the horses veered sharply into the other, dumping its unfortunate rider into the dirt. A loud groan went up in the crowd for the fallen horseman, followed by a cheer and applause as the remaining horseman triumphantly raised the looped ring above his head.

"I think there's a power vacuum since Schmidt's problems," Rico speculated, "and Torres is trying to move in."

"But isn't Esmeralda filling the vacuum?" Dennis wondered.

"Maybe," Aurelia answered. "But the situation is fluid. She's probably only a caretaker of the position. She's not ruthless enough to take absolute charge of all of Gerhardt's operations."

"Doesn't that put her in danger?" Dennis wondered.

"Somewhat," Aurelia answered. "But she knows how to play her hand carefully. If Torres moves in, she'll step aside for him. Plus, she has his affection as a trump card."

"How serious is his bid to take over?" Dennis peered intently at his mom. "Does he have a realistic chance?"

"Nobody knows for sure," his mother answered. "It probably depends on you, in part."

"On me?" Dennis shot a glance at her. "On me?" he repeated. "What the hell do I have to do with any of this?"

"More than you think," his mother answered.

"You're his natural son," Rico interjected, "and Schmidt sent you here, didn't he?"

"Is that what this trip is about?" Dennis asked, his mouth dropping open. "Boy, I must be naive; I thought I was here to gather evidence for his trial in Chicago."

"Maybe you are," Rico answered, "but you can't blame Torres and everyone else around here for thinking that you were sent here as his heir apparent."

"Holy shit." Dennis lowered his face into his hand. "Can you believe this? Me, taking over Schmidt's international crime syndicate?" He let out a forced laugh.

"Don't underestimate the danger you are in," his mother cautioned. "Torres can be rough."

"Was he the son of a bitch who set up the car ambush?" Dennis shouted. "That fucking bastard."

"I don't know," his mother answered.

"One thing I can tell you for sure," Rico commented, looking at Dennis, "our room here is bugged."

Dennis looked curiously at Rico.

"When they moved my bed out of the room, I saw the listening device in the wall, just behind the headboard."

After the Race of the Rings, everyone convened in an area behind the main building where a tent had been erected. The festivities, including food, music, and dancing, continued there. A fogón (bonfire) was started nearby and many of the gauchos gathered around it. They shared asado (barbecue), drinks, and conversations that became more animated as the evening wore on.

Journeymen musicians from Buenos Aires assembled into a band. They played traditional songs that everyone sang to and tango music that people danced to. The non-stop drinking and festivities since early afternoon had lowered everyone's inhibitions and enveloped them into a care-free spirit of animation and merriment. Several couples were engaged in heated arguments and two reseros, who'd had a few too many drinks, got into a scuffle before the others broke them up.

Dennis and Rico were feeling no pain. They even teased Sandoval and Montoya into downing some local drinks. Aurelia, Dange, and a number of the middle-aged women had gathered into smaller circles of conversations about their children, their husbands, and their household chores.

Since the activities had largely been concluded, Esmeralda began to relax a little and circulated among the guests. She stayed away from the gauchos around the fogón, though; they had become too rowdy.

After a while she settled in closer to Dennis and Rico. The conversation started out as an explanation to Dennis of the local traditions and customs, and became more personal as the music continued to play. Dennis's mother glanced periodically at her son and Esmeralda. After a while Dennis asked Esmeralda to dance when the musicians switched to a slow ballad.

"I can't help commenting," Dennis said, holding Esmeralda at arm's length, "how beautiful you are."

"Thank you," Esmeralda answered.

"Of course, you must be used to those compliments by now."

"It is still nice to hear them," Esmeralda said, "especially if they are sincere."

"It's hard to imagine any compliments to you that wouldn't be."

"Most are, but not all of them. Sometimes there is jealousy, or even anger."

"I guess I can understand that. Some women—and some men, for that matter—might be intimidated by your beauty."

"But tell me about yourself, Dennis," she said, shifting the conversation. "It must have been difficult to be taken away from your mother at such an early age."

"It wasn't easy."

"You handled it well. It looks like you turned out to be a nice person."

"I'm not sure about that. I'm pretty good at acting."

"Well, I am certain the hurt went deeply. Has seeing your mother again after all these years helped?"

"It's helped. I'm not sure it has resolved all the issues, though. I still have a few left, including the ones with Gerhard Schmidt."

"He is your father."

"It'll take a while to accept that."

Esmeralda didn't say anything. She continued to dance with Dennis, relaxing in his arms a little more. When she did, Dennis drew her closer.

"I think," Dennis said, "you know him better than I do."

"Yes, I do," Esmeralda answered quietly, almost in a whisper.

"Would it be inappropriate for me to ask you what kind of man he is?"

"The man he is, is not the man he was when we first met."

Dennis thought about how Schmidt stopped seeing his mother after he met Esmeralda and felt a surge of anger.

"The man you met, was he the same when my mother first met him?" he asked, tightening his grip on her.

Dennis felt Esmeralda tense up in his arms.

"I'm sorry," Esmeralda said. "It must be painful for you. I can understand that you would be angry."

"No, *I'm* sorry," Dennis said, pulling back a bit and looking at her. "I have to learn how to deal with this. I can't blame you for Gerhardt's behavior."

"I'm sure there's enough blame to go around." Esmeralda relaxed again. "I can assure you that I am far from perfect."

"He seems to want me to get involved with his operations. Did he tell you why?"

"No, he didn't. But then I learned early in our relationship not to ask him certain questions."

"What about your relationship with him?"

"It's complicated."

"Does he love you?"

"I don't know."

"Did you ever ask him?"

"I did. Once."

Dennis was silent.

"I asked him whether he loved me," she went on. "At first he was taken aback. Then he became angry. He told me never to ask him that again."

"And you could live with that, with that kind of a non-answer?"

"I guess I can. I learned long ago, when I was still in my early teens, that life is not black and white, that it has many ambiguities."

"Do you think he loves you, even though he never told you so?"

"I think so, although it is not necessarily like the romanticized 'true love' we like to believe in, like we see in the movies. It is more like a mixture of love and need—like most relationships, I guess."

Dennis remained silent for a while. He thought about his relationship with Linda. Was it love, or need, or some mixture of the two?

"How about you, Dennis?" Esmeralda asked, pulling away slightly to look at him. "Are you in any relationship?"

"Somewhat," he answered. "I have to admit, though, that it's also ambiguous."

"What is she like?" Esmeralda pressed on.

"She's intelligent and caring…"

Dennis felt a hand grab him by the shoulder and yank him around hard. A fist flew into his face and smashed him between his right eye, cheek and nose. He felt an explosion go off in his head as he fell backwards toward the ground with a thud.

The music stopped. The women in the crowd fell silent and turned to the dance floor. The gauchos sprinted away from the fogón and formed a circle around the scuffle. Their eyes were ablaze with excitement and anticipation.

Sandoval and Montoya leaped from their seats and pushed their way onto the dance floor. They grabbed Torres by each of his arms as he looked down on Dennis.

"You bastard," Torres shouted at Dennis, trying to free himself from Sandoval and Montoya. "You son of a fucking whore! Go back to where you came from!" He made a violent movement to free himself from the two men, but they overpowered him.

Rico stood up from his seat and watched carefully for any sudden movements from the circle of gauchos. He unbuttoned the top three buttons of his shirt and put his right hand inside. He unsnapped the leather strap of his holster.

Esmeralda knelt down beside Dennis and tried to comfort him. He was groggy, but conscious. Blood was seeping from his nose and mouth. His mother reached over and put a blanket under his head. She asked Dange to fetch some ice.

"All right," Rico said, breaking into the circle and addressing the crowd. "I think we've had enough excitement for the night. I think it's time for everyone to go home."

"Who the hell are you?" Torres shouted, struggling to free himself from Sandoval and Montoya. "Who are you to tell everyone to go home? I'm in charge of the ranch here, not you!"

The gauchos stirred restlessly. They weren't ready to go home yet, either. They wanted to see a fight, maybe get in on the action.

Esmeralda stood up and addressed everyone. "The festivities are over. Thank you all for participating."

CHAPTER 9

CALUMET RIVER

Norm Stackley was a careful young man. He didn't drink or carouse with the guys from his Bridgeport neighborhood, at least not very often. After high school he focused on getting an accounting degree from UIC and commuted every day from his home where he was the third of five children of a blue-collar Irish American family. He got a job at a manufacturing plant right after he graduated from UIC, but continued to study nights to prepare for the CPA exam. After that, he enrolled at the John Marshall Law School in Chicago for the evening classes and got his law degree in four years.

He was hired by the Engstrom law firm after he passed the bar exam and learned how to do things the Engstrom way. He worked his way up, one step at a time, until he became a partner. After several more years, he became an equity partner from sweat equity and from the money he contributed to the law firm using the personal savings he had managed to accumulate over the years.

One day in January 2000, Norm got a call from the US Attorney's office in Chicago. They asked to meet with him to discuss an IRS audit of the Omniglade Foundation. Norm had prepared all of its tax returns and knew that the audit hadn't gone well. He brought Shaun Williams along, just in case the IRS's civil audit was converted to a criminal case.

He was interviewed by Phil Klein, although Donna Stevens, Roman Kaminski, and several IRS agents were also present. Klein's office was on the sixth floor of the Dirksen building. It was small, cramped with papers, and had a noticeable absence of any decorum. Klein did have several small snapshots of his children though, taped to the metal shelving above his desk.

Klein made no attempt at small talk. He sat straight in his swivel chair and began with the evidence the IRS had gathered against the foundation. It showed serious irregularities, he said, including evidence of financial involvement with a political campaign, a prohibited activity for a tax-exempt organization.

"At the very least, it could mean the revocation of the foundation's tax-exempt status," Klein said.

Norm remained silent. He knew enough to keep quiet when potential trouble was brewing. Besides, Shaun would have cut him off in mid-sentence if Norm so much as uttered anything even remotely connected to the audit.

"It looks like you were deeply involved with the preparation and maintenance of the foundation's books and records, as well as its nine ninety tax returns," Klein went on, "so you could face criminal prosecution, at least as an accessory."

"I'd have to see what evidence you have," Shaun interjected.

"If Mr. Stackley is indicted, he'll be entitled to all the evidence in our possession."

"Even if there is some alleged evidence against the foundation, Norm did the accounting part of it—he didn't audit its books."

"Maybe so, but we have even bigger issues here. It looks like some of the money coming into the foundation is from abroad."

"So what?" Shaun said. "The foundation gets donations from all over the world."

"So we're also looking at possible money laundering. Accessory to that kind of involvement is a serious felony."

"I think you're fishing," Shaun said. "If you had that kind of evidence there would've been an indictment already."

"We're building a case—several, maybe—and we'd like Mr. Stackley's cooperation."

"What kind of cooperation?"

"We're willing to recommend lesser charges against Mr. Stackley in exchange for his cooperation in gathering additional evidence to tie Kevin Engstrom's congressional campaign to the foundation."

"I'll have to talk to my client."

"We're also interested in Mr. Stackley's cooperation with regard to the Schmidt case."

"Even if we would entertain any so-called cooperation, the biggest problem we have is the attorney-client privilege. The law firm was retained by both the Omniglade Foundation and Mr. Schmidt, so Mr. Stackley is legally prohibited from violating their attorney-client privileges."

"Mr. Stackley's involvement in both of those cases was as an accountant, not as an attorney, and therefore the attorney-client privilege wouldn't apply."

Shaun Williams was taken aback by that tactic.

"That's quite a reach, Mr. Klein," Shaun managed to respond. He hadn't heard of that approach when he worked there.

"I think we can make a case for that," Klein said. There was no inflection in his voice.

If he's bluffing, Shaun thought, *he's pretty good at it. I wouldn't want to face him in a poker game.*

"We'll get back to you," Shaun concluded.

He and Norm Stackley walked out of the Dirksen building and headed to the indoor parking garage nearby. It was already after four thirty in the afternoon and turning dark. Norm was shaken and pale. Shaun suggested they have a drink and talk about this serious turn of events.

"Do you want to stop in at the Union League Club?" Shaun asked. "We can have an early dinner there and a drink."

"I could use a drink," Norm answered, "but I don't want to run into anybody I know right now. I'm not in the mood for social chatter."

"It was just a suggestion."

"Yeah, thanks," Norm caught himself. "I like the idea. I'd just rather go somewhere else, that's all."

"Well, I can suggest the South Side, around Hyde Park, maybe. I know the area."

"That sounds better."

"I don't mean to sound facetious," Shaun went on with a slight smile, "but you won't run into too many people you know there."

"I guess the South Side has become predominantly black." Norm offered a weak smile.

"Yeah. Many of the well-to-do whites who settled the area originally fled to the suburbs after the influx of blacks from the South in the early part of the century—even the liberal ones."

Shaun stated it matter-of-factly; Norm didn't sense any anger or animosity in his voice. He remained silent. He wasn't sure he wanted to get into that conversation right now.

"It's one thing to favor equal rights for the blacks in the abstract," Shaun went on, "but another to live next door to them and send your kids to the same school."

"Yeah, that's pretty much the history of the South Side," Norm agreed. "You went to law school there, didn't you?"

"Yes, the University of Chicago. I know some of the hangouts there."

"Let's do it," Norm agreed. "You drive."

They got into Shaun's Chrysler and headed out to Lake Shore Drive. Norm fell silent again. He was clearly worried. Shaun was respectful of that and waited for Norm to speak.

"You also live on the South Side, don't you?" Norm finally broke the silence.

"Yes, in the Kenwood District."

Shaun parked the car when they got to Hyde Park and Norm followed him into a neighborhood tavern. It was still early enough that it wasn't overly crowded. They ordered sandwiches and drinks.

"You think Klein's bluffing about the attorney-client issue?" Norm asked, taking a good gulp of his scotch on the rocks.

"I'm not sure. It's a pretty aggressive posture for the US Attorney to take, but it could be a gray area."

"I suppose we should consult with an attorney who knows the law regarding attorney-client privilege."

"Make sense to me."

"If Klein has a strong argument against the attorney-client privilege, I'm in deep trouble."

"That's a tough one," Shaun agreed, taking a hefty bite of his Reuben sandwich.

"I either cooperate with Klein, or I go to jail."

Shaun remained silent, eating his sandwich.

"I might go to jail either way," Norm observed.

He ordered another scotch on the rocks. He called his wife Barbara on his cell phone.

"Hi, Barb. I'm gonna be a little late tonight. Something came up at the office. The kids OK?"

He listened while she talked.

"Yeah. Go ahead with dinner without me. I love you."

Norm put away the cell phone and bit into his BLT sandwich. Shaun excused himself and went to the bathroom.

After a few minutes, two men walked up to Norm. One was short, about five feet ten, but muscular. The other one was big, about three hundred pounds.

"Hi," the short one spoke. "I'm Paco. This is my friend Mario."

Norm seemed taken aback. "Yes?" he asked hesitantly. "Can I help you?"

"We want you to go with us," Paco said. "We have a car waiting outside."

"What? What for? Where's Shaun?"

"He got delayed," Paco said, coming closer to Norm. Paco placed his right hand inside his jacket lapel. The big guy came closer and stood directly in front of Norm.

"We need for you to go with us now," Paco said. "You can take the sandwich with you."

Norm became uneasy and frightened. He turned to look behind him. The few people in the bar didn't seem to notice what was going on. They were watching the evening news on TV, or talking to the bartender. The waitress wasn't anywhere to be seen. Shaun never came out of the bathroom, or wherever he went to.

Norm stood up slowly and followed the men out the door. He left his unfinished BLT sandwich and the second scotch on the table. When they walked outside, the big man reached into Norm's shirt pocket and took out the cell phone. He then led Norm into the back seat of the car that stood double-parked by the front door of the bar. He sat down with Norm in the back seat; Paco took the wheel. There was a click as Paco locked all the doors from his control panel.

"Where are you guys taking me?"

"We're going to do some sightseeing," Paco said. "The South Side's nice this time of the year."

"Look, guys, if you want money, I'll give you everything I've got."

Norm rummaged through his pockets and came up with several hundred dollars.

"Here," he said, offering it to the big man. "I can arrange to get some more."

The two men were silent as the car turned south on to Stony Island Avenue. It was dark already, although Norm could see the lights of the local neighborhood stores through the tinted windows as the car whizzed by.

"Look guys, I have a wife and two kids. One is heading to college in the fall—the boy. What is this about? I wanna make it right. Anybody I can talk to about this?"

They remained silent.

"Does this have anything to do with Schmidt?" Norm went on, trying to break through to them. "I can talk to him about this. I can make it right."

The lights on Stony Island Avenue disappeared after a while. Norm could make out shadows of large buildings; they appeared to be warehouses. He was vaguely familiar with the street. It was part of the Port of Chicago area where he had represented a company that wanted to establish a facility at the Lake Calumet terminal. He remembered that Stony Island Avenue dead ended into the confluence of the Grand Calumet River and the Little Calumet River, just south of the Dead Stick Pond.

The wheels crunched as the car came to a halt in front of prairie grass that had sprouted by the water. They opened the door and let him out. It was windy and cool. Norm shivered and had a strong urge to piss. He opened his fly and began to urinate. Two shots, muffled by a silencer, popped into his body. Norm slumped to the ground and lost consciousness. Some snow flurries drifted down and settled on his inert body.

CHAPTER 10

EMBASSY RECEPTION

It was New Year's Eve, Friday, December 31, 1999, the dawn of the third millennium. For a good number of the six billion people alive on earth that day, it was a big deal. Some of the religiously faithful prayed in churches or retreats and paid homage to the founder of Christianity. A number of over-the-hill hippies left over from the baby-boomer generation holed up in solitude with cannabis cigarettes and water bongs to await the end of the world, while groups of geeks and computer techies in Silicon Valley braced for an apocalyptic crash of millions of computers due to the Y2K bug. Most people, however, just wanted to go out and party.

At ten o'clock that night, dressed in black tuxedos they had just rented, Dennis and Rico got out of the Land Rover they had arrived in for the New Year's Eve party at the US embassy on Avenida Colombia in the Palermo section of Buenos Aires. It was modest transportation compared with the black limousines and flashy sports cars of the other guests. They joined the line at the gate waiting to go through the security manned by several uniformed Marines. To avoid complications, Rico had left his Beretta with Sandoval, who drove off with Montoya in the Land Rover. They parked by a café on Avenida del Libertador where they ordered mate and waited to be called for the ride back.

The main ballroom was filling up rapidly with the elegant crowd. The din of the simultaneous conversations was pierced gently by the thin strains of the string quartet playing *Eine kleine Nachtmusik*, a serenade for strings in G major, by Wolfgang Amadeus Mozart. Ambassador Buzz Bixby, a successful businessman and generous contributor to Bill Clinton's presidential campaigns, was at the head of the reception line, accompanied by his daughter, Amanda, as well as several functionaries from the embassy.

"Welcome to Buenos Aires." Ambassador Bixby extended his hand to Dennis. "I hope your stay here will be more pleasant than the ride from the airport."

Dennis smiled and thanked the ambassador for the invitation. He went on to greet Amanda and the others in the reception line.

"Thank you for your quick action, Mr. Monzoni," Ambassador Bixby greeted Rico, "and for bringing my daughter back safely."

Dennis and Rico headed over to the bar, picking up a few hors d'oeuvres as they passed the waitresses circulating with trays. Dennis ordered a glass of Malbec from the Mendoza region and turned to Rico.

"Looks like a pretty big event," he said, taking a sip from his glass.

"It's the annual New Year's eve schmoozing with the doers and shakers of Buenos Aires," Rico explained. "It's especially big this year because of the millennium."

"I'm surprised we got invited. We're not exactly doers and shakers, here."

"I think the ambassador wanted to show his appreciation for bringing his daughter back safely from the airport."

"Thanks to your quick action."

"How are you doing with the lessons at the gun club here?"

"I'm getting the hang of it."

The five members of a popular young band from England began to assemble their equipment on a stage that was set up in the main ballroom. They were on a world tour and happened to be in Buenos Aires. Amanda liked them and had asked her dad to invite them to play at the New Year's Eve party. During their breaks, a local band played tangos and other dance music. The music, the dancing, and the alcohol combined to loosen up the guests and the party was in full swing by the time midnight arrived.

Rico's Globalstar satellite phone rang. He took it out from the inside of his jacket pocket, extended the antenna, and answered.

"Hi. It's Linda," the voice on the other end said. "Is Dennis there?"

Rico handed the phone to Dennis.

"Happy New Year," Linda said. "We miss you."

"Happy New Year to you," Dennis answered, walking to the patio outside to get away from the noise, "although you have a couple of hours to go yet in Chicago."

"Yeah, it's ten o'clock here. We're at Kevin's house for the occasion, but the mood's a little somber tonight."

"Oh? What's going on?"

"Norm Stackley's disappeared. Neither his wife Barbara nor dad have heard from him in the last two days."

"That's weird."

"Norm called Barbara Wednesday, about six in the evening, and told her he was going to be late. That was the last anybody's heard from him."

"That's not like him to just disappear. Have the police been notified?"

"Dad called them this morning, after we tried everything else."

"That's scary. Barbara must be beside herself. How's she doing?"

"Not very well, as you might imagine. We asked her to join us here at Kevin's house, but she declined. She said she wants to be home with the kids."

"I don't know what to say. Tell Barbara we're praying for her and the kids, and for Norm's safe return."

"Thanks. I'll tell her. How about you? Are you OK there in Argentina?"

"Yeah, we're OK. We're at a New Year's Eve party at the US embassy."

"Sounds glitzy."

"I guess it is, but I don't know too many people here. I'm basically just getting sloshed on the local wine."

"Rico must know some people there," Linda brightened up slightly. "His family's from there, isn't it?"

"Yeah, he introduced me to a few people."

"I wish I could be there with you."

"Yeah, me too. Well, anyway, thanks for calling. Let me know if you get any news about Norm."

Dennis shut off the phone and remained quiet for a while. The revelry of the party was muted with the patio door closed. He became conscious of the delayed thuds of fireworks that were being set off on the near horizon. Dennis glanced up from the patio and caught a few explosions that crowned, faded, and then died gracefully. He looked higher and gazed at the stars in the dark and cloudless sky. He wasn't familiar with the southern hemisphere, but it felt peaceful to look into the window of that part of the universe.

He looked around the patio and noticed that it extended into a lovely garden. He felt a tug to remain there for a while. Then the patio door opened and a woman walked toward him. She looked familiar.

"Hi," she said. "Do you remember me?"

Dennis peered closer through the dim light. Then a smile of recognition lit his face.

"Oh, yes. We met at the film seminar at the Chicago Bar Association. Lori, Lori De Luca, isn't it?"

"Yes, but I have a confession."

Dennis looked at her quizzically.

"I'm not Lori De Luca," she said.

Dennis's smile faded as he continued to look at her. She wore a simple but elegant evening dress and had a modest smile.

"My real name is Donna Stevens and I work for the US Attorney's office in Chicago."

Dennis wished he'd brought his wine with him to the patio.

"And before you say anything, I have to tell you that I've been assigned to the Schmidt case. Any of your legal involvement in the matter is adversarial to mine."

Dennis wasn't sure how to respond. "I guess that explains why you're here."

"I feel ethically bound to disclose my role in this since our legal paths are likely to cross again," Donna went on.

"Duly noted," Dennis responded. He touched the silver medallion hanging around his neck. "I won't raise that issue if it comes up in court."

Dennis had an urge to walk away, but he hesitated. Even though the situation was ambiguous and unsettling, it would be impolite, he decided. He also felt a weird tug to see where this was going. He glanced briefly at Donna, waiting for her to continue.

"Look," Donna exhaled. "I'm sorry to have deceived you. I won't blame you if you're upset." Her apology sounded sincere.

"Confused," Dennis conceded, "more than upset. Taken aback, maybe." He eased up on his voice. "I presume you were doing your job."

"I was, but I didn't feel very good about it."

"I guess I can deal with that. It hasn't been the first surprise since I got here."

"You're letting me off too easily."

"I appreciate honesty. Look," Dennis decided to take the initiative, "if it's all the same to you, why don't we drop this and have a drink? I think I need another one."

"Me too," Donna nodded.

They walked back inside the ballroom and ordered drinks at the bar. The party was still in full swing, although a few of the older guests were starting to leave. Dennis nodded to Rico, who was huddled in a circle of Argentinean businessmen.

"I heard about the incident from the airport," Donna changed the subject. "Everybody's talking about it at the embassy."

"Yeah, one of the drivers was killed."

"That was unfortunate. It could've been a lot worse, I imagine."

"Thanks to Rico, it wasn't."

Donna took a sip of her wine. She looked around and saw Roman Kaminski. They had arrived together. He was sharing a drink with several of the Marines, who were dressed in marine blue social evening uniforms. Roman glanced back at Donna and raised his eyebrows slightly, a subtle signal to see if she was OK. Donna parted her lips into a slight smile.

Donna looked back at Dennis. "I hope I'm not getting too personal," she said, changing the subject again, "but I was wondering if you've had a chance to meet your mother."

"Yeah," Dennis answered briefly. He wasn't sure he wanted to talk about it. Donna looked quietly at Dennis, hoping he would continue. Dennis downed his wine and looked back at her to see if she was up for another one. She nodded. Dennis caught the bartender's eye and raised two fingers.

"I haven't fully processed it yet," Dennis went on. "She explained why she sent me away from Argentina. It seemed reasonable, under the circumstances."

"It's hard for me to imagine any circumstances that would justify a mother giving up her five-year-old son for adoption."

"You're not the only one. But I was lucky, I was adopted by a very nice family."

"Maybe you were, but I'm not sure how I would've handled it in your situation."

"You learn to survive. If it doesn't kill you, it makes you stronger, they say." Dennis allowed his mouth to form into a weak smile.

"That's a glib cliché." Donna sounded like a teacher scolding a student.

The bartender brought over the two glasses of wine. Dennis pulled out a five dollar bill from his pocket and put it in the tip jar. The bartender seemed pleased.

"My real mother is very nice," Dennis went on. "It was weird, but nice, to connect with her again. She has a heart of gold."

"My psyche would've been scattered into a thousand pieces if I'd gone through that."

Dennis glanced at Donna again. Either she was really sympathetic, or she was getting sloshed, like he was. He felt like he was getting on a roll.

"It wasn't so much seeing my mother again after all these years," he said, "as finding out who my real father is."

"What? Another surprise?"

"Yeah. Bigger than you think. It's Gerhard Schmidt."

"Holy shit!"

"Yeah."

"I don't know if you've heard," Donna added, "but Schmidt's been arrested in Chicago this morning."

Dennis looked at Donna without speaking. He wasn't sure how to react to this latest twist.

"He was picked up at O'Hare," she went on, "as he was trying to board a flight to Argentina."

"I hadn't heard yet," Dennis blurted out. He ordered another round of drinks for them.

The crowd was thinning out. The rock band on tour had disbanded and the local group was playing a slow number, something resembling a foxtrot.

"Look," she said, "I'm probably jeopardizing my job, but would you like to dance?"

He held her close as they danced. She melted into his arms.

"I was attracted to you from the first time we met," Dennis spoke softly to her.

Donna gave him a reassuring squeeze.

"That was when you were still Lori De Luca." Dennis pulled his head away slightly to glance at her with a hint of a smile. "I hope that wasn't part of the act."

"I had a hard time keeping the act going," Donna whispered, without looking back at him.

They continued to dance quietly.

"You know, Dennis," Donna spoke again, "you're involved with some dangerous stuff. I'm afraid you're going to get hurt."

"I know. I feel like I've been caught up in something out of my league."

"I wish I could tell you more," she said, "but I've compromised my job already."

"Don't say any more. I'll try to work things out."

CHAPTER 11

METROPOLITAN CORRECTIONAL CENTER

Dennis Brunt led his brother Marko from the indoor parking garage in the Loop to the corner of Clark and Van Buren Street where MCC, the Metropolitan Correctional Center, was located.

"That's a weird-looking building," Marko observed.

"Yes, it's triangular," Dennis explained. "It rises to twenty-eight floors and there's an exercise area and basketball court on the roof for the inmates."

They went through security in the lobby and then took the elevator to the visitors' room on the eighth floor. They sat down and waited for Gerhard Schmidt, who had been held there without bond since being picked up at the international terminal of O'Hare Airport as he was boarding a LAN flight for Argentina on New Year's Eve.

"Thanks for coming with me," Dennis said to Marko.

"No problem," Marko replied. "I guess he's my father, too."

"He hasn't been much of a father to either of us," Dennis observed, looking out over the large visitors' room, which was starting to fill up with other visitors and inmates.

"I think you got the better end of the deal when you left Argentina," Marko noted dryly.

"I didn't know him as a father, or as anything, when I left. What was he like with you?"

"I barely saw him."

"Was Mom around?"

"Yes, I lived with her, but she was working all the time. I learned how to take care of myself."

"Didn't he support you financially?"

"I don't know. He never claimed paternity, for you or me, so I don't know that he had to support us."

"Did Mom ever push the issue, legally, I mean?"

"I don't think so. My guess is she was too afraid to piss him off and lose whatever support she was getting."

"I hope we can begin to piece things together in some way."

"I don't know if there's any way."

"We share family blood. We'll find a way."

"We've grown up in different worlds, you and me. The father we share has been arrested and is awaiting trial. He'll be imprisoned, probably for the rest of his life."

Dennis and Marko turned and saw Gerhard Schmidt entering the visitors' room. He was dressed in the regulation orange jumpsuit and blue tennis shoes. He sat down next to Dennis and Marko.

"This will not last long," Schmidt said. His voice was controlled.

"You mean our meeting?" Dennis asked.

"No, this," he said, waving his arm in the general direction of the visitors' room.

"You mean the incarceration?"

"The incarceration, the arrest, all of this misunderstanding."

"You've been here almost three months and they denied your bond request," Dennis said.

"Williams has filed an appeal."

"You're too great of a flight risk," Dennis added. He tried to look at Schmidt with objectivity. That was difficult, but for a powerful man who had lost his freedom, Dennis thought Schmidt would have shown more anger.

"Williams has requested the judge to reconsider the denial of a bond," Schmidt went on. "He will argue that the government has no evidence that I am a flight risk."

"The only problem with that argument," Dennis interjected, "is that you were boarding a plane to leave the country when they arrested you."

Schmidt remained silent, almost stoic. Dennis wanted to get through that façade, that veneer of stoicism. He wanted to get inside this man's head.

"Why do you want me to get involved with your operations?" Dennis asked, changing the subject.

"Because your brother Marko is incompetent," Schmidt blurted out. There was frustration in his voice.

Marko stiffened visibly.

"He is a drug addict," Schmidt sneered with disdain.

Marko remained silent, although his eyes blazed with anger.

"He is your son, like I am." Dennis made an effort to soften the angry rhetoric.

"What kind of a son is he?" Schmidt asked dismissively. "He disappointed me."

Marko bolted up from his chair. "Who are you to make judgments about *me*?" he shouted. "You were never part of our family. You were a father in name only!"

Some of the visitors in the room turned to look at the rising commotion. Two guards approached cautiously.

"Please," Dennis said softly, turning to Marko, "let's not dredge up the past."

Marko sat down again. "I wish we could have spent more time together," Dennis continued, looking at Marko. "I really looked up to you when we were growing up in Buenos Aires."

"Your mother prevented that," Schmidt interjected, speaking to Dennis. He didn't look at Marko. "She is the one who pleaded with me to send you away."

"Why did she do that?" Dennis challenged Schmidt.

"Because she is an ignorant and stupid woman," Schmidt retorted.

"She told me that she wanted a better life for me," Dennis said, trying to protect his mother. "She said she didn't want me growing up in the streets like Marko."

"Marko was not strong enough to survive in the streets of Buenos Aires."

"I could've ended up the same way," Dennis objected.

"Perhaps. But there was only one way to find out. You survived in America, did you not?"

"That's not the same thing," Dennis tried to reason. "Mr. and Mrs. Brunt took care of me. They adopted me and treated me like their own son."

"I made sure that you never lacked for anything."

"You mean you helped them financially?"

"Of course, the way I would have if you had remained in Argentina. The point is, you do not know what you can survive until you are forced into it."

"Is that what you wanted for your children, a survival test?"

"If you wish to call it that," Schmidt grumbled. His eyes looked cold and hard.

Dennis remained silent. He didn't know what to say.

"You are naive to believe that the world is fair," Schmidt went on. "You either learn to survive, or you fall by the wayside."

Dennis remained silent for a while longer. Their worlds seemed so far apart. The gap between them was so huge he didn't even know where to begin.

"My father, Klaus, had to start from nothing when he came to Argentina after the war. He had to leave everything that was his behind in Germany: his wife, his children, his prestigious position as a military officer."

"I didn't know that," Dennis's voice softened. "I'm so sorry. It must've been rough for him—and for you."

Schmidt hesitated for a moment. He seemed surprised by Dennis's observation. His eyes lost their hardness for a moment, almost imperceptibly, but then it passed in an instant, as fast as it had appeared.

"Spare me the sympathy," Schmidt blurted out, his voice dripping with sarcasm. "It sounds condescending."

Dennis fell silent again.

"How can I help now?" Dennis asked, changing the subject. "What is it that you want me to do?"

"The St. Lawrence Seaway will open as soon as the ice melts on the Great Lakes in late March," Schmidt went on. "I have a shipment that is ready at the Iroquois Landing Terminal. I need you to make sure it gets out."

"What shipment?"

"You do not need to know the details. The proper shipping documents will be with the Yugo Import/Export Company. Sign them and Yugo will know what to do after that."

"I don't want to get caught up in your operations."

"I need you now. You are my blood. You have a duty to your father."

"I'm not sure I buy that rationale."

"Then do it for Marko and your mother. You will help them if you do this."

Dennis remained silent, conflicted.

"Morley Engstrom has prepared my power of attorney for you," Schmidt continued. "I already signed it. He, Williams, and Monzoni are involved in this operation and they will help you to execute it."

CHAPTER 12

FUND RAISER

T he crowd in the ballroom at the Palmer House on Adams Street in the Chicago Loop was elegant. Most of the men wore business suits while their spouses, or dates, wore evening dresses. The unmarried career women circulated in dark business suits with skirts either above or just below the knee, depending on how socially aggressive they wanted to be that evening. A few local entertainment and professional sports figures circulated throughout the ballroom, surrounded by media types and/or groupie hangers-on. Their casual and trendier counter-establishment attire was evidence that they had "made it."

It was Tuesday evening, March 28, 2000. The event was the kick-off fund-raiser for Brian Hannigan, who was there to announce his candidacy for Governor of Illinois. Close to four hundred people paid twenty-five hundred dollars each—twenty-five thousand for a table of ten. A few of the heavy hitters contributed fifty thousand, which included a private, one-on-one audience with Hannigan before the official program began.

Although Morley Engstrom usually supported Republican candidates, he was savvy enough to read the tea leaves and supported the candidates he needed to support, regardless of their political affiliation. He was among those who paid fifty thousand for a private audience with Hannigan. Since his personal attendance at the Democratic event would have raised eyebrows, he sent ten people from the law firm, headed by Shaun Williams, who was, in fact, a registered Democrat. Dennis Brunt was also there, along with Rico Monzoni, Linda Engstrom, and others from the law office, including Joe and Myrtle Brunt. Their political affiliations, if any, were more ambiguous.

Shaun was on his cell phone with Morley Engstrom. "When you go in to see Hannigan," Morley instructed him, "see if you can get him to drop the case against the Omniglade Foundation."

"Check."

"Also feel him out about Schmidt, if you can."

"That's a little dicier."

"Tell him we're prepared to make additional contributions to his campaign in the future."

"How much are we talking about?"

"Don't be specific. Make it clear, though, that it'll be substantial if he's willing to negotiate."

"I doubt that he'll be willing to talk about an active case, especially Schmidt's."

"Just ask. The worst that can happen is he'll say no."

"It's too big of a case right now," Williams went on, "and he's counting on getting a lot of political mileage out of it."

"Don't beat around the bush with him," Engstrom insisted. "He's been around and knows how the game is played."

Shaun and Dennis Brunt went into a separate room where Hannigan was greeting the big donors privately. They waited politely until Hannigan was ready for them.

"Hi," Hannigan said, reaching out to Williams. "Thanks for stopping by."

"We're excited about your candidacy for governor," Williams responded with a handshake, "and wish to offer our support."

"I appreciate that. You're with the Engstrom firm, aren't you?"

"Yes."

"How's Morley doing?"

"He's fine, thank you. He sends his personal regards."

"Morley's a war horse from the old school," Hannigan said, smiling broadly. "We've locked horns several times in the past."

"Yes sir. I understand you do go back a way."

"I've been hearing some nice things about you, Shaun," Hannigan said, changing the subject. "They say you're an up and comer in the Chicago bar."

"Thank you. This is Dennis Brunt," Shaun said, introducing Dennis. "He's taken over some of the tax work at our law firm now."

"Yes. I heard about the mysterious disappearance of Norm Stackley, the head of your tax practice. Is there any further word on that from the Chicago police?"

"Not yet, but we'd like to discuss with you some of the issues he was involved in."

"Sure, absolutely," Hannigan said, turning quickly to Klein, who was standing nearby. "Talk to these two gentlemen, Phil. I have to go into the main ballroom. I think the program is about to start."

Klein nodded and led Williams and Brunt into an anteroom, next to the coat rack.

"We're just wondering about settlement in the Omniglade matter," Williams spoke first.

"OK. Here's the deal," Klein responded. "Omniglade loses its tax-exempt status and Kevin Engstrom drops out of the Republican primary."

"That's pretty drastic."

"With the evidence we've got so far, I'd say that's a generous offer."

"I'm not sure about the evidence you've got, but without Stackley's testimony at trial, your case against Omniglade gets a lot weaker."

"Maybe. But do you really want us to get involved in his disappearance?"

"Can you leave Kevin Engstrom out of the deal? He's got a good shot at winning the primary."

"No deal. If Clayton or the media get hold of some of the contributions made to his campaign, he's gone anyway. He's damaged goods."

"Morley will be disappointed."

"Do you want us to get into Kevin's knowledge of these contributions?" Klein asked, starting to lose interest in the conversation.

"What about Schmidt?" Shaun asked, trying to get that topic in while he still had the chance. "Can we talk about that?"

"Not a chance."

"Isn't there any room for negotiation? We're prepared to be very flexible, and generous, on our end."

"You can't be flexible enough." Klein turned to leave. "I've got to get back into the ballroom."

After Klein left the anteroom, Shaun turned to Dennis.

"Morley will be disappointed," he said.

Dennis remained silent.

"What do you think?" Shaun asked him.

"About what?"

"About this," Shaun barked, irritated at the outcome of the negotiations. "Don't be disingenuous."

"I don't think I have the stomach for this kind of stuff."

"Welcome to the real world, sonny."

Shaun called Morley on his cell phone as they walked into the main ballroom, and conveyed the government's offer to him. Dennis sat down at the Engstrom table between Linda and Rico. Linda turned warmly to him as the waitresses started to bring in the salad plates.

"How did it go?" she asked.

"Not good." Dennis's response was perfunctory. He wasn't in the mood to talk about it.

Jeff Dunston, a motivational speaker and radio talk show host, stepped up to the podium. He was the master of ceremonies that evening.

"Good evening, ladies and gentlemen!" he greeted the crowd enthusiastically, with a beaming smile that displayed a set of symmetrical white teeth. "Welcome to the Brian-Hannigan-for-Governor event."

The lilt in his voice rose to a higher crescendo. "It's a wonderful turnout for the *next Governor of Illinois*!"

The crowd responded with enthusiastic applause, commensurate with the lilt in his voice.

"As the delicious food is being brought to your tables, I'd like to recognize several of the honored guests in attendance this evening."

"I could use a drink," Dennis said, turning to Rico.

"Me too," Rico said, sliding back his chair.

"Can I get you a fresh one?" Dennis asked Linda.

"Yes, I'll take a Merlot," Linda answered.

Dennis and Rico walked to the bar section and joined the back of one of the loose lines. Three bar staff, including two attractive waitresses, took rapid-fire drink orders that fueled the adrenaline of the high-energy crowd milling about, talking, shaking hands, and greeting acquaintances and friends—or would-be friends. The glass tip jar, placed prominently in the middle of the bar, was overflowing with green bills. Rico ordered a scotch on the rocks for himself and two Merlots for Dennis and Linda. "So what does the Schmidt case look like now?" he asked, turning to Dennis.

"Hannigan won't deal," Dennis stated bluntly.

"That puts Schmidt's operations in jeopardy," Rico observed darkly. "The wolves in Argentina have been circling around them."

"You mean Torres?" Dennis glanced at Rico.

"Yeah, him and his cronies."

"Good luck to them."

"You don't think you can have an impact on that?"

"What do you mean?"

"I mean that Schmidt wants you to get involved."

"Yes, but I want no part of it."

"I could help out. I have a lot of contacts there. Engstrom and Williams are in on it, too. We can put a team together."

"Let me think about it."

"You'd be crucial in getting all the levers of the operation from Schmidt, especially in Argentina. They see you as Schmidt's blood and are more likely to follow you if Schmidt is not there. Schmidt trusts you."

"What about Torres and Esmeralda?"

"I think that Esmeralda could be part of the team, if you want her to be."

As they moved back toward their table, they ran into Donna Stevens and Roman Kaminski, who were heading for the bar. Dennis caught Donna's eye and his mood brightened. She was dressed in a navy blue business suit, an appropriately professional look for the evening, although she was still clearly feminine. Dennis liked that about Donna.

"Well, hello," Donna said, turning toward Dennis. It was a soft hello, almost a question mark.

"Oh, hi, Donna," Dennis answered, trying to deal with the social moment. "I thought I might see you here. Have you met Rico Monzoni?"

"It's a pleasure to meet such a beautiful lady," Rico gushed, turning on his Latin charm. He reached for Donna's right hand and kissed it gallantly.

Donna was pleasantly disarmed at Rico's affectionate declaration. He seemed sincere and she smiled.

"Although we haven't been formally introduced before, I believe we're not total strangers," Rico went on, smiling graciously.

Donna glanced quizzically at Rico.

"I believe you attended the New Year's Eve party at the American embassy in Buenos Aires," Rico explained, "just a few months ago."

"Yes," Donna responded, "we were there, Mr. Kaminski and I. I didn't realize you were there as well, Mr. Monzoni."

"I was there with Dennis, who you know, of course, but I didn't have the pleasure."

Dennis looked away in an effort to avoid the thread of the conversation.

"Well, I'm happy to make your acquaintance now, Mr. Monzoni," Donna added. "Please meet Roman Kaminski," she said, turning to Roman.

After the introductions, there was a slight pause. Dennis turned to Donna again.

"I presume Hannigan plans to resign his position as US Attorney now that he's thrown his hat into the governor's race."

"Yes," Donna answered.

"I'm going to excuse myself," Rico said, turning to go. "I'll take the other wine glass back to our table," he added, taking it from Dennis's hand. Roman excused himself as well.

Donna glanced at Dennis briefly. "Hannigan asked me to be on his campaign team."

"Oh?" Dennis was caught by surprise. "What are you going to do?"

"I'm thinking about it," Donna said. "It means that I would have to resign my position, as well."

Dennis looked at Donna, waiting for her to continue.

"It would solve the problem of compromising my objectivity in the Schmidt case," Donna declared.

Dennis looked down remorsefully. "Look, I'm sorry I got you involved with me. It was my fault."

"I wasn't exactly ambushed into it."

"I feel responsible. It seems like I've screwed things up pretty badly."

"Don't be so hard on yourself."

"Everything is happening so fast." Dennis downed his glass of wine.

"It's a dangerous game. Please be careful."

Dennis remained silent for a while, absorbed in thought.

"As usual, I'm focused on myself," he said in an attempt to lighten the mood. "Can I get you a drink?"

Dennis ordered two more glasses of wine. The bar crowd had thinned out and most of the guests were already seated at their tables. The salad dishes had been cleared away and the waiters were bringing in cups of lobster bisque. From a distance, Linda glanced in Dennis's direction. Donna noticed it and turned to Dennis.

"Maybe we should head back to our tables," she said.

"Wait," Dennis hesitated.

Donna took another sip of wine.

"I feel like I can trust you," he went on.

Donna looked at Dennis. It seemed like a nice thing to say, but she wasn't sure whether it was intended to be personal.

"That's a scary thought," she said, with a hint of a smile.

Dennis leaned closer to Donna and spoke in a low voice. "I've been hearing about a shipment of goods from the Iroquois Landing Terminal. I don't know all the details yet, but it's going to be very soon."

Donna nodded.

CHAPTER 13

IROQUOIS LANDING TERMINAL

10:12 p.m., Wednesday, March 29, 2000.

Morley Engstrom gazed up from the dock at the Iroquois Landing Terminal on Lake Michigan, near the mouth of the Calumet River, at the gantry crane that loomed like a giant praying mantis above the tractor rig with the twenty foot TEU shipping container. The burly longshoreman operating the crane guided its claws around the container and then hoisted it over to the deck of *Dansk Göteborg*, a Danish cargo ship. Rico Monzoni, Shaun Williams, Dennis Brunt, and Marko Castillo, Dennis's brother, huddled next to Morley Engstrom in the strong shadows cast by the glaring shaft of light from the gantry crane. They raised their coat collars and stiffened with the penetrating gusts of cold air from Lake Michigan.

"This whole area along the lake and the Calumet River used to be mostly steel mills, railroad tracks, and grain elevators," Engstrom mused as he watched the delicate handling of the cargo container. "My grandfather was injured not too far from here in 1937, in the Memorial Day Massacre."

"I remember reading something about that," Williams picked up the thought. "What happened?"

"He used to work for Republic Steel. Some union was trying to organize the workers and Republic Steel didn't take too kindly to that."

"How did he get hurt?"

"He was picketing in front of Republic Steel's main gate on One Hundred Sixteenth Street when the police arrived and opened fire."

"The workers didn't have too many rights in those days."

"He got shot, but he was lucky. Ten men died."

Another rig with a TEU intermodal container box pulled up and was hoisted by the crane operator onto the ship.

"This is the last one," Engstrom said, turning to Williams. "Make sure the teamsters and the stevedores get paid."

"I thought the export company took care of those details."

"This is a special job that we're handling off the books. There are no invoices. The union guys get paid in cash."

"I'll take care of it with the stewards. The bill of lading is going with the captain, though, right?"

"Correct. Take it up to him."

Williams climbed up the gangplank of the ship, followed by Rico, Dennis, and Marko. They made their way through the jagged deck passage and climbed up to the bridge located on the top of the superstructure, near the aft of the 565 foot container ship. The inside of the bridge, Dennis noted, was as wide as the ship, but narrow and cramped with modular desks and electronic equipment. Even though it was the nerve center of the ship, its design was utilitarian. The slight feeling of claustrophobia was abated, though, by the large window panels along the entire front of the bridge. Once the ship is afloat, Dennis surmised, your eyes could rest on the panoramic view of the deck below and the broad horizon of the water ahead.

The captain was sitting on one of the swivel chairs in front of the modular desk equipped with LED lights and the small arc of a wheel that controlled the ship's direction. Three other men stood nearby, facing the windows. They turned to look at the visitors. Dennis and Rico recognized Hector Torres, as well as Paco and Mario, two of Schmidt's muscle men here in Chicago. Torres held a gun in his hand and pointed it in the direction of the visitors.

"Thank you for bringing us the bill of lading," Torres said. "We'll need it when we reach port in Albania."

"Torres!" Williams exclaimed. "What are you doing here?"

"We're here to protect our shipment," Torres replied calmly.

"Your shipment? You're crazy, Torres!" Williams shot back. "This is way over your head."

"Your head is the one at risk, Mr. Williams," Torres added with dry sarcasm. He waved his gun in a signal to have them come in closer, but off to one side. "I need that bill of lading from you, Brunt."

Dennis hesitated, but then carried it over to Torres.

"Look, Torres," Williams interjected, "you're going to screw it all up."

"Shut up, Williams!"

"This kind of deal takes a lot of coordination," Williams went on, "and the right contacts. You can't do it by yourself."

"That's why you're going on the trip with us, Williams, you and your cohorts here."

Torres signaled the captain to start the engines. The captain pushed some buttons and the ship shuddered with the throbbing of the powerful engines below deck.

Williams, Rico, Dennis, and Marko exchanged glances. Rico edged closer to the exit.

"Paco," Torres ordered, "you and Mario search our guests. Remove all items from their possession."

As Paco and Mario moved toward the group, Rico bolted out the exit.

"After him!" shouted Torres. Paco and Mario drew their pistols and gave chase. Several shots could be heard from outside.

Torres became visibly nervous and agitated. "Don't try anything funny," he said, waving his pistol at the others. "Paco and Mario will find him—or bury him in the lake. He has no place to hide on this ship."

"Go ahead," Torres said, turning to the captain.

The captain issued orders to the crew via the radio. Ropes holding the ship to the pier were released and the vessel started to glide slowly away. Several tug boats with search lights chugged into position and began to guide it into the open water of Lake Michigan.

"When Schmidt gets word of this," Williams went on, "you won't find a place to hide."

"Schmidt is done for," Torres smirked, "and so are you."

Without warning, the ship slowed and glided to a stop. Torres shot a glance at the captain. "What is happening?" he asked nervously.

The captain shrugged. "The tug boats seem to have disengaged," he said. The ship's radio crackled and came alive.

"This is the coast guard," a voice announced. "Inform the captain that all engines are to stop and the gangplank is to be lowered for our boarding."

Torres stiffened and pointed his pistol at the captain. "Turn on full power!" he shouted. "We're going."

"You're crazy, Torres," the captain retorted.

"Do as I tell you!" Torres shouted, waving the gun at the captain.

"Where are you going to go? We're on a lake."

"We're heading to the Atlantic Ocean, captain," Torres ordered. "Just like the original plan. Now *go!*"

The captain throttled the engines to full power and the ship began to gain momentum. The radio crackled again. "You are ordered to stop! Do not go forward!"

"Keep going!" Torres ordered the captain. "What are they going to do, torpedo us?"

The ship continued to pick up speed.

"Look, Torres," the captain tried to reason with Torres. "Even if you could outrun them—which you can't—the St. Lawrence Seaway has a number of canals and locks. The authorities can stop you from going through them."

"Not if they value your life—and the others."

The ship's radio crackled again. "This is Commander Hargrave of the US Coast Guard." The tone sounded more conciliatory. "I'd like to speak to the captain of the *Dansk Göteborg.*"

"This is Hector Torres," Torres spoke, picking up the microphone. "I'm in charge of this ship."

There was a moment of silence, and then Hargrave spoke again.

"I see. What is your intention, Mr. Torres?"

"My intention is to get safe passage for this ship to the Atlantic Ocean."

"We're concerned for the safety of all the crew and passengers," Hargrave replied.

"They will be safe if you don't try to interfere."

"I understand."

"How long will it take us to get to the Atlantic Ocean?" Torres asked the captain.

"About a week, but it could take longer."

"You're the captain," Torres bristled. "You're supposed to know how long it will take."

"The lakes just opened up for shipping after the winter months, so there could be some backup traffic at the locks."

After a few minutes, the ship's engines shuddered and stopped. Torres's agitation and nervousness rose to a new level.

"Captain, I order you to go forward!" he screamed. "Go, I tell you. *Now!*"

"The engines are not responding to the controls here," the captain answered.

Torres got on the radio with the coast guard. "I'm holding four hostages on the bridge, Commander Hargrave," Torres shouted. "If you don't let us go through, I will shoot them one by one."

"We are not detaining you," Hargrave answered. "I repeat, the ship has stopped without our interference."

As Torres faced the radio, Marko Castillo edged closer to Torres. He lunged for the gun and grabbed it. The gun went off and a bullet tore into Marko's shoulder. Williams and Brunt rushed Torres and stifled him. Williams managed to yank the gun from him. Torres backed off, alone now and without a weapon.

"Sit down on the floor, Torres!" Williams barked. "Any sudden move from you and this gun goes off again."

"The man who ran out," the captain observed, "he must've found his way down into the engine room and got the engineer to throw the main power switch."

"Yeah, that's Rico," Dennis said. "He's got a gun, but so do those two goons chasing him. I've got to help him."

Just then, Marko swooned and pitched forward. Dennis jumped and caught him around the waist before he fell to the floor. Blood was oozing out of his left shoulder. Dennis helped Marko into the captain's chair and held him in place.

"Hold on to him," the captain said to Dennis. "I'll dress his wound in a second. Let me secure this son of a bitch first."

As Williams trained the gun on Torres, the captain took out a set of handcuffs from a cabinet, yanked Torres's arms behind him, and handcuffed his wrists. "Keep an eye on him," he said to Williams.

The captain then took out a first aid kit and started to dress Marko's wound. "Hang in there," he said to Marko. "We'll try to get you medical help as soon as possible."

The captain got on the radio to the coast guard. "This is the captain speaking. Is Commander Hargrave there?"

"Hargrave here. Go ahead, captain."

"I have the bridge under control now. We are also holding one of the hijackers, but two others are loose on the ship and they're armed."

"Can you lower the gangplank?" Hargrave asked. "We can get some men up there to help you."

"I'm not sure. I don't know whether my crewmen are safe. I'll see what I can do."

"Are you OK to sit by yourself?" Dennis asked Marko.

Marko nodded.

Dennis filled a paper cup with water from the five gallon water dispenser and handed it to Marko. He then took out his Beretta and slipped out the exit. His plan was to see if he could hook up with Rico. Based on what had happened, he figured Rico might be in the engine room, or somewhere nearby.

It was after midnight already and pitch black, other than some spotlights from the ship, and the waning crescent moon. The gusts of wind were more aggressive at that height. He climbed down carefully, one step at a time, through the alternating stair ramps from the top of the bridge, keeping an eye out for Paco and Mario.

He wasn't sure whether he could find his way to the engine room, especially in the dark, but he figured if he kept going down he would eventually find a door to go below deck. He stopped momentarily, took out his cell phone, and speed-dialed Rico. It didn't work; he had only one or two bars on his cell phone and he wasn't sure if Rico had any reception at all below deck, if that was where he was.

As Dennis climbed down to the main deck, shots rang out. The bullets pinged ominously nearby and ricocheted off the hard metal surfaces. He pressed his back against part of the superstructure and peered over his shoulders. He spotted two shadows further down in the container hold. Several more shots were fired from their direction.

Dennis's cell phone rang. It was Rico.

"I'm coming up the stairs into the container hold area," Rico whispered. "I've got a glimpse of Paco and Mario. I don't think they've seen me yet. Keep firing at them and keep them occupied. I'll try to get closer."

"Got it."

Dennis leaned out slightly and fired two shots toward Paco and Mario. They returned fire. Rico crept up within a few feet of Paco and fired a shot into his back, chest high. At the same instant, Mario, who was standing close to Paco, spun around violently. Rico knocked him out with a hard pistol blow to the head. Mario collapsed to the ground, unconscious and bleeding. Paco gasped a few moments, blood spurting out of his chest, and let out his last breath.

Several uniformed men with pistols climbed up the gangplank. They advanced cautiously in a crouch.

"Hold your fire!" Dennis shouted in their direction. "The three kidnappers have been disabled and the ship is under control."

Commander Hargrave stepped forward and assessed the situation.

"Those two on the deck are two of the three kidnappers," Rico said. "One of them is dead."

"The third one is on the bridge with the captain," Dennis added. "He's not a threat any longer, although one of our men has been shot and needs medical attention."

Just then Phil Klein climbed up the gangplank, followed by Roman Kaminski and Donna Stevens. Kaminski, who had his gun drawn, was followed by several other armed FBI agents.

"I'm seizing this vessel for the government," Klein said, approaching Commander Hargrave. "Here are the court papers, signed by a magistrate of the district court."

"This is a crime scene under our jurisdiction," Commander Hargrave responded, "but we'll be happy to turn this over to you once the forensic work is done."

Dennis came closer to Donna. "Thanks for following up with this," he whispered. Donna returned his gaze, but remained silent.

CHAPTER 14

AURORA COUNTRY CLUB

The morning of April 23, 2000, broke clear and brilliant. Dennis put on his tan summer suit with matching suede shoes and socks and drove to the Aurora Country Club for the traditional Easter brunch.

The main dining room filled up rapidly with club members, their families, and their guests. The youngsters flitted about hyperactively while the adults circulated, greeting each other in the holiday spirit and in the merry mood of a gorgeous spring day. It took a while to corral everyone around the large table that had been reserved for the Engstrom group. Once they had settled down, though, they got in line and served themselves, brunch style, from the row of sumptuous food islands that included poached eggs Benedict, sausages, bacon, ham, fruit, pancakes, quiche, shrimp, smoked salmon, salads, as well as vegetable dishes, desserts, and breadstuff. The more adventurous ordered hot roast beef carved by a chef from the shank under the heat lamp, as well as mimosas, Bellinis and bloody marys.

In between bites of food, several conversations were going on simultaneously. Shaun Williams, who was seated next to Kevin Engstrom and his wife Beverly, asked Kevin what his plans were now that he had dropped out of the Republican primary race for his congressional district.

"I'm going to take some time off to think about it," Kevin answered.

"There are a few other opportunities besides the congressional district," Shaun ventured. "You've gotten some good public exposure so far and still have a surplus in your campaign fund."

"I'm not sure that public office is the right path for me."

"Officially, you dropped out of the race for personal reasons," Shaun observed, "so there hasn't been any damage done in the eyes of the public."

"Maybe so," Kevin mused, "but the US Attorney can play rough."

After the last of the brunch dishes had been cleared away by the staff, the men from the Engstrom table migrated to the bar and lit up cigars. Morley Engstrom raised his scotch glass and announced that Joe Brunt, wanted to make an announcement.

Joe Brunt eased up to the front of the group and cleared his throat. "Thank you," he began tentatively. "As you may know, I've been with the firm for thirty five years; thirty five happy years—the last ten as a partner."

Some of the men nodded; others murmured sounds of encouragement.

"But Myrtle and I aren't getting any younger," he continued. "It seems like we've been discussing—more and more, lately—the idea of doing some traveling."

The group fell silent, attentive.

"So I'd like to announce my retirement."

He took a sip of his scotch, then continued. "Morley and I discussed this and we've agreed that my retirement would be effective as of June thirtieth."

"We'll be sorry to see you go," Morley stepped up and put his arm around Joe's shoulder. "We appreciate everything you've done for the firm, Joe, especially for the real estate practice, and you deserve this."

"I'd also like to announce," Joe continued, "that I'm passing on my partnership position, and my equity stake in the firm, to my son Dennis."

"Hear, hear!" the men raised their drinks in a toast to Dennis.

"Myrtle and I love Dennis very much," Joe went on. "He's been a wonderful son to us—God's gift to us, I would say—since we adopted him almost thirty years ago."

"Speech, speech!" The men raised their drinks in a toast to Dennis. Dennis sipped his Benedictine on the rocks, but declined. The men then broke off into smaller groups as Dennis was ushered into the one with Morley, Kevin, Scott Peterson, Shaun, Joe, and Rico.

Morley was the first to speak. "Schmidt's trial is scheduled for next month," he said. "His chances of getting off are slim to none. Am I right about that, Williams?"

"Pretty much," Williams replied.

"His operations have taken a hit, but they still survive," Morley went on. "What do we know about them?"

"Torres is toast," Rico commented, "but Esmeralda is managing to hold on to whatever pieces are left."

"What's our game plan?" Morley asked. It was an open question, although he turned slightly toward Shaun Williams.

"A lot depends on Dennis," Shaun said, turning to Dennis.

"You've got to make a decision, Dennis," Kevin said. "Are you in or out?"

"What am I getting into?" Dennis asked.

"We can pick up the pieces of Schmidt's operations," Rico said, "but we don't have all the levers. You're the only one Schmidt seems to trust."

"I'm not sure about getting involved in Schmidt's operations," Dennis said, wavering.

"You don't have to get involved with them," Morley went on. "We just want you to get us the details we need from Schmidt."

"We'll take it from there," Kevin added.

"How can you consider taking over an operation that's so dirty, so criminal?" Dennis blurted out in frustration. "At the very least, you're running the risk of getting into legal trouble, both here and in Argentina."

"Maybe some parts of it are not pristine," Morley interjected, "but no business is."

Dennis took another gulp of his Benedictine.

"Look," Morley went on, "we don't want to get involved in any criminal enterprise any more than you do. We just want to pick up the remaining pieces of a loose and disorganized infrastructure with significant potential."

Dennis remained silent.

"We'll restructure it into a tight and legitimate operation," Morley went on. "The law firm stands to gain from that."

"It's a win-win proposition," Williams added.

Dennis walked outside alone, holding on to his drink. He downed it and felt the soothing numbness of the buzz.

"You don't have to do it if you don't want to," Joe Brunt said, approaching Dennis. "You don't owe anything to the law firm, or to Schmidt."

"Is it true that Schmidt sent you money for my support?"

"Yes, he did, from time to time. We never asked for any, but we accepted it."

"Did he attach any conditions to the money?"

"Not that I know of. Actually, we never spoke to Schmidt about it."

"You just accepted the money he sent to you?"

"The money was sent to Morley and Morley deposited it into our personal account."

"How is it that you and Myrtle came to adopt me in the first place? How did you know about me?"

"As you know, Myrtle and I were childless in our marriage. Myrtle couldn't have any. So Morley asked me one day if we would be willing to adopt a five-year-old boy from Argentina. He must've been contacted by Schmidt about it."

"I thought it was my mom, Aurelia, who wanted to get me out of Argentina; I thought Gerhardt was opposed to that."

"I don't know the details. I was just told by Morley what flight you were on and I went to pick you up. After that, we did all the paperwork to get you adopted legally. We worked with an attorney in Argentina to get legal clearance from that end of it."

"It sounds like Gerhardt and Morley set this whole thing up. I feel like I've been manipulated my whole life."

"You could walk away from everything," Joe Brunt observed pensively. "You could cash out your equity stake in the partnership and start over."

"I thought about that," Dennis replied, "but it's not that simple. Aurora is my mom and Marko is my brother. I can't just abandon them. They're my blood."

Joe Brunt nodded sympathetically.

"And, for better or worse, Schmidt is my father."

"Look. You're not Mother Teresa," Joe Brunt added. "You've started a new life here in America. You can't be looking over your shoulder with a guilt complex."

Just then, Linda walked up to the two of them. "Are you OK?" she asked Dennis.

"No, I'm not OK," Dennis answered, somewhat brusquely.

"Do you want to get away from here?" Linda asked. "Just you and me."

"I don't think so. I want to be alone for now. I have some thinking to do, some decisions to make."

Dennis turned and walked to his car. He turned on the ignition of the BMW E46 coupé and headed toward I-88, the East–West Tollway. He wasn't sure where he was going and didn't care. He turned onto the ramp heading west and just opened it up to about eighty miles per hour. There weren't too many cars on the road. He was glad.

I think Linda is part of this whole setup, he thought to himself. *The attention, the affection, the connection to Schmidt. I don't know who to believe any more.*

The speedometer started to pass ninety and was still climbing, although Dennis wasn't aware of it. *I don't even know who I am,* he thought as his mind continued to race along with the car.

Then the cell phone rang in its cradle on the dashboard. He let up on the accelerator and pushed the button to answer the call. "Hello," he said, not really in the moment, "who is this?"

"Hi," a voice came through the speaker. "It's Donna."

Dennis started to focus on the voice. "Hi," he said.

"Happy Easter."

"Uh…Happy Easter," Dennis answered.

"I was wondering what you were doing," Donna said.

"I don't know what I'm doing," Dennis said without sarcasm. "I'm just driving on I-88."

"Are you alone?"

"Yeah, really alone."

Donna was silent.

"Thanks for calling," Dennis said. "Your voice is the nicest thing I've heard all day."

"Come pick me up," Donna said. "I'll go for a ride with you."

"That sounds good," Dennis said. He eased up on the accelerator and then got off at the next exit. He turned left and got back on I-88 heading east toward Chicago.

CHAPTER 15

MCC²

Dennis pulled up to the curb of Donna's high-rise in the Streeterville section of Chicago, put on the blinkers, and scooted into the spacious lobby. Donna was chatting with the security man behind the desk and turned with a pleasant smile when she saw Dennis.

"Hi," Dennis smiled back at Donna, giving her a light hug and kiss on the cheek. They walked out into the street.

"I left the Easter brunch early," Dennis said, holding the car door open for Donna.

"What happened?" Donna asked, slipping into the front seat. Dennis walked around to the driver's side and got in.

"Joe Brunt is retiring," he said, "and they've offered me his partnership."

"Congratulations!" Donna beamed.

"Yeah, but it comes with baggage," Dennis said, glancing back at Donna.

"What kind of baggage?"

"They want to pick up the pieces of Schmidt's operations and they want me to be a part of it."

Donna fell silent. The clicking sound of the car's blinkers filled the void.

"Can't you take the partnership without the Schmidt mess?" she asked.

"It seems to be a package deal," Dennis said, starting the engine.

A lone Chicago policeman walked up to the car and tapped on Dennis's window. Dennis pushed the button to lower it. The policeman didn't look too happy.

"There's no parking here, sir," he said pointing to a sign on the sidewalk. "You'll have to move on."

"Thank you, officer," Dennis responded. *He's probably not too happy about having to work on Easter Sunday,* Dennis thought. "We're leaving right now."

Dennis shifted into gear to go, but his mounted dashboard phone rang. He put his foot on the brake and pressed the answer button.

"Schmidt wants to see you," Rico's voice was on the speaker. "Where are you?"

"I'm in Streeterville, with Donna."

"Can you run over to the MCC right away?"

"Shit. It's Easter Sunday."

"Schmidt says it's urgent. I'm here with him."

"What does he want?"

"I don't know. He said you're his attorney and he wants to see you."

Dennis turned to Donna. "Do you have any other plans?"

"I'll change them."

The policeman was tapping his night stick into his palm. Dennis took his foot off the brake and stepped on the gas pedal.

● ● ●

Dennis and Donna went through security at the Metropolitan Correction Center and then took the elevator to the eighth-floor visitors' room, where they met up with Rico.

"What's this urgency about?" Dennis asked. He was annoyed with Rico and with Schmidt.

"I don't know," Rico answered, "but he seemed nervous and upset."

"I would be too, if I had just lost an entire cargo container shipment," Dennis observed dryly.

The room was filled with other inmates, as well as visitors who came to see them. Several guards, interspersed throughout, eyed the area. Gerhardt Schmidt walked in. He was dressed in the regulation orange jumpsuit and blue tennis shoes. *I guess they make the prisoners wear those garish colors so they're easier to spot,* Dennis observed silently. *Either that, or the authorities want the prisoners to be properly humiliated.*

"Thank you for agreeing to see me on such short notice," Schmidt said, approaching Dennis and Donna. "Happy Easter."

Dennis was surprised by Schmidt's cordiality. "This is Donna Stevens," he said, introducing her to Schmidt. "As you may know, she was previously with the US Attorney's office and assigned to your case."

"It's a pleasure to meet you, Ms. Stevens," Schmidt said, turning in her direction. Donna didn't offer her hand. Schmidt gave a slight bow and sat down.

"What did you want to see me about?" Dennis asked.

"I'm afraid that I didn't act much like a father to you, or to Marko, the last time we met here," Schmidt continued in the softer tone.

"Marko was injured on the cargo ship," Dennis answered. He wanted to be angry and blame Schmidt for what happened, but it would have sounded harsh, given Schmidt's polite tone. "He'll be in the hospital for a few more days."

"Yes, very unfortunate," Schmidt went on. "You and Rico are to be commended for your brave action."

"Torres and his goons tried to take over the shipment," Dennis said, waiting to see where Schmidt was going with this.

"My incarceration made Torres greedy," Schmidt commented. "He saw an opportunity to take over my operations."

"I'm not sure how much is left of your operations," Dennis observed, "although Engstrom and some of the staff want to pick up the pieces."

"There are more pieces than you think," Schmidt said.

Suddenly, two men barged into the visitors' room through the door to the stairs. They brandished weapons.

"Everybody down on the floor!" a man with an Uzi submachine gun shouted. Dennis recognized him. It was Arturo Sandoval. The other one, Alejandro Montoya, held a pistol. They had been Dennis's bodyguards in Argentina.

The inmates, the visitors, and the guards turned toward the two armed men and froze in silence. Sandoval and Montoya burned with intensity as they scanned the room, alert for even the slightest movements.

"Everyone down on the floor!" Sandoval shouted again, even louder. "Now!"

The inmates, the visitors, and the guards sat down, or squatted on the floor. Schmidt signaled Rico, Dennis, and Donna to gather into a circle with him.

"Face down!" Sandoval ordered the others.

Montoya waded into the crowd sprawled on the floor and disarmed the guards. He threw their pistols into a large duffel bag he carried.

"Hey, man," a black inmate stood up suddenly as Montoya passed him. "Take me with you."

Montoya wheeled and struck him hard with the butt of his pistol. The inmate collapsed on the ground, blood oozing from his head. The guards flinched, but didn't move.

"Out this way!" Sandoval signaled the Schmidt circle, pointing back to the door.

Montoya flung the door open and ran into the stairwell, followed by Schmidt, Rico, Donna, and Dennis. Sandoval followed behind, facing the guards in the waiting room, brandishing his Uzi. Once in, they quick-stepped behind Montoya, who rushed up the twenty floors to the recreation area on the roof, back up the way they had come down. Sandoval stood at the top of the first flight of stairs, watching the door. A few seconds later it was flung open by other guards with weapons. Sandoval strafed them with a round from the Uzi. The guards rushed back inside and shut the door again. They called the other guards down in the lobby and warned them of the escape.

Sandoval sprinted the twenty floors up to the roof and caught up with the others. A helicopter waited for them, its rotors flip flopping in idle. As soon as they scrambled in, the pilot gunned the engine and the helicopter swooped up and away, heading north.

Dennis and Donna huddled close together in adjoining jump seats, next to Rico. Schmidt, Sandoval, and Montoya sat in the opposite jump seats. Sandoval and Montoya held their arms at the ready.

"This is crazy." Dennis looked at Schmidt. "You're such a big target there's no chance you can pull this off."

"My chances are much better with the two of you for company," Schmidt answered.

"Let Donna go," Dennis pleaded. "Take me as your hostage."

"That is noble of you, son," Schmidt looked at Dennis with cold eyes, "but two hostages are better than one. You two are my safe passage to Argentina."

• • •

Phil Klein got a call on his home phone from FBI agent Roman Kaminski. "Mr. Klein," Kaminski spoke urgently, "we have an emergency."

"What's up?" Klein asked. He held off from taking the next bite of the hamburger he held in his other hand.

"Schmidt has broken out of the MCC."

"Shit!" Klein dropped the half-eaten burger on the kitchen counter. "What happened?"

"He escaped by helicopter from the roof of the MCC," Kaminski reported. "He took some hostages with him, including Donna Stevens."

"Is anyone chasing them?"

"One of our helicopters got airborne within ten minutes, but we haven't been able to spot them yet."

"Anything on radar?" Klein asked.

"Negative," Kaminski responded. "They must be flying below radar."

"Meet me at the MCC," Klein barked.

• • •

Schmidt's helicopter landed on the tarmac at the Palwaukee Municipal Airport in Wheeling, next to one of the fixed base operators there. A Learjet was parked nearby, its engines humming in idle. Dennis recognized it as Schmidt's private plane, the one that had flown him and Rico to Buenos Aires several months before. Rico had previously explained to Dennis that it was a Bombardier Continental with two Honeywell turbofan engines and that it could push to 540 miles per hour at an altitude of forty-five thousand feet.

They scrambled out of the helicopter and clambered hurriedly up the plane's stair ramp. Dennis stooped to enter into the fuselage, although he could walk fully erect once inside. There were four seats on each side of the aisle, arranged in two quadrants of facing pairs. Dennis and Donna were ushered to the pair of seats in the rear, facing front. Schmidt sat in the seat facing back, opposite Dennis. Rico, Sandoval, and Montoya sat in the quadrant of seats ahead and buckled up for the flight.

The cockpit door in the front was open. Captain Arroyo was seated at the controls while Antonio Mendoza, the navigator, sat to his right. There was no flight attendant this time.

Arroyo got on the radio and informed the control tower that he was ready to take off.

"You're cleared for runway sixteen thirty-four," the radio chirped back.

Arroyo taxied the plane to the edge of the five-thousand-foot runway and then gunned the engines. Dennis felt his chest push back against the seat as the Learjet curved gracefully into the sky, heading south. He reached across the aisle for Donna's hand and gave it a light squeeze.

Once they reached cruising altitude, Schmidt stood up and helped himself to a drink from the kitchenette in the galley. "We will arrive in Caracas in approximately five hours," he said. "After refueling there, we will continue to Buenos Aires."

"Look, Mr. Schmidt," Donna spoke up, "even if the air force doesn't shoot us down before we leave US territory, I suspect that the federal arrest warrant will be honored by any of the Interpol countries, no matter where you go."

Schmidt took a sip of Cointreau on the rocks he had poured into a tumbler and approached Donna. "I'm sure, Ms. Stevens, that Interpol will receive and disseminate the arrest warrant throughout its network of one hundred ninety participating countries, but, as you should know, it has no jurisdiction to make arrests. It depends on the law enforcement agencies of the individual countries to enforce it."

"We have a long-standing extradition treaty with Venezuela," Donna countered. "You could get arrested when we land there for refueling."

The Cointreau on the rocks eased into his bloodstream and Schmidt allowed himself a casual smile. "I believe you are correct again, Ms. Stevens." Schmidt enjoyed the verbal sparring with an intellectual equal, especially when he had the advantage. "As you may know, however, Hugo Chavez was just elected President of Venezuela last year. I do not believe he is enamored of America and its capitalist form of democracy."

Captain Arroyo summoned Schmidt to the cockpit. "A Mr. Klein is on the radio. He asked to speak with you."

Schmidt took the radio. "Schmidt, this is Phil Klein," the radio crackled. "We're concerned about the safety of the passengers on your flight."

"They are safe for now," Schmidt responded, "as long as you do not make any stupid moves to interfere."

"I understand," Klein continued. "I want you to know, however, that I'm authorized to negotiate the terms of your return for trial."

"Hah," Schmidt let out an involuntary laugh. "You should have negotiated those terms when I was under your control at the MCC."

"Roger that," Klein's voice came through. "Obviously, the situation has changed."

"I have no desire to return to your jurisdiction," Schmidt added.

"You must realize," Klein went on, "that, from here on, your movements and your business dealings will be tracked closely. The scope of your activities will be severely curtailed."

"I will manage, Mr. Klein," Schmidt said. "But thank you for your concern."

Klein made another effort to negotiate. "You may know that we currently have an extradition treaty in place with Argentina. It becomes effective in several months, on June fifteenth, I believe."

"I plan to speak about that to the staff of Mr. Fernando de la Rua," Schmidt stated flatly. "You may know that he is the President of Argentina."

"Very well," Klein answered. "We'll discuss your situation with Buzz Bixby, our ambassador in Buenos Aires. He will keep us apprised of your activities."

"It is reassuring to know that you care about my activities, Mr. Klein," Schmidt concluded. He handed the radio to Captain Arroyo and headed back to the kitchenette. He poured himself another Cointreau.

"What are your plans for us?" Dennis asked.

"That depends on you," Schmidt answered. "At least in part."

"Look, Gerhardt," Dennis's voice took on a tone of determination, "I'm not going to join your operations in Argentina."

"Do not be so serious, Dennis," Schmidt said. His voice was calm, bordering on friendly. "We will discuss this further. Please help yourself to a drink while I change out of these prison clothes. They are very unpleasant."

Donna glanced at Dennis. "I'll take a Cointreau," she said. She didn't want Dennis to lose his cool.

Rico stood up from his seat in the other quadrant and walked over to the galley. "I'll get that," he said. Sandoval and Montoya glanced over, but remained seated.

"Are you in on this, too?" Dennis turned to Rico in disappointment. "I guess I'm not a very good judge of people."

Rico didn't say anything. He poured the drink and handed it to Donna. He remained standing by the kitchenette until Schmidt came out of the bathroom.

"This feels much better," Schmidt said. He was dressed in khaki slacks, suede shoes, a matching tan shirt, and a blue blazer. It looked like a stylish ensemble for an evening party on a yacht. Rico handed Schmidt his drink.

"This is all a game to you, Gerhardt, isn't it?" Dennis blurted out. He resented Schmidt's seeming joviality.

"Perhaps it is all a game, as you say," Schmidt replied. "You have one last opportunity to join the team."

"You want me to join a criminal operation?"

"You have many good qualities, my son," Schmidt went on, sitting down again on the seat in front of Dennis, "but street smarts, as they say in America, is not one of them."

"So why do you want me?" Dennis retorted with anger.

"You are my blood."

"I don't deny that you're my father, but you don't need me."

Schmidt placed his drink in the cup holder. "If you cannot be persuaded directly," his tone became somber, "perhaps you can be persuaded indirectly. Please hand me a pistol, Mr. Monzoni."

Dennis and Donna stiffened in their seats. Dennis reached across the aisle and took hold of Donna's hand again.

Rico walked over to the other quadrant and unzipped the duffel bag on the floor, next to Montoya. He took out two pistols. He placed one inside his jacket and carried the other one over to Schmidt. Sandoval and Montoya stood up and faced the unfolding drama.

"Perhaps you feel that you have other options," Schmidt said slowly as he waved the pistol gently in the general direction of Dennis and Donna. "Perhaps your relationship with Ms. Stevens has emboldened you, given you a sense that you may not need the law firm and the team that goes with it. Perhaps you have acquired more independence than I had planned. I had not counted on you developing this relationship with Ms. Stevens."

Captain Arroyo opened the cockpit door. "We have an escort," he said, "an F-16."

Schmidt glanced out the window to confirm. "They will not shoot us down," he commented. "We have too many innocent people on board."

"Please be careful with the pistol, Mr. Schmidt," Arroyo warned. "If it goes off it could pierce a hole in the fuselage and we would experience rapid decompression."

"Unfortunately, Ms. Stevens," Schmidt went on, ignoring the warning from Captain Arroyo, "you have chosen the wrong person to bond with. Your choice conflicts with mine."

Donna stood up and flung her unfinished drink at Schmidt. The remaining alcohol and ice cubes splattered on Schmidt's face and jacket.

Schmidt rose and struck Donna across her face with the pistol. Dennis jumped at Schmidt, but he was restrained by Sandoval and Montoya. Rico drew out his pistol and handed Schmidt some napkins from the kitchenette. Donna sat back down on her seat. Blood seeped from a cut on her right cheekbone.

"Your show of bravado is a useless gesture," Schmidt said to Donna, wiping his face and jacket with the napkins.

"It's all about control," Dennis spat out the words at Schmidt. "You say I'm your blood, but that's meaningless. There's no love to put meaning into those words. It's all about control."

"Love is a function of control." Schmidt looked coldly at Dennis. He turned the pistol toward Donna. "My plans were proceeding in the right direction until you interfered, Ms. Stevens."

Dennis strained against Sandoval and Montoya. "I will never, never join your dirty, filthy operation!" he shouted. "I would rather you killed me!"

Schmidt sat down in the seat facing Donna. He raised the pistol and aimed it toward her chest.

"Goodbye, Ms. Stevens," Schmidt spoke calmly. "If the bullet goes through your chest, it will lodge in the backrest of the seat. That will ease the concern of Captain Arroyo."

Suddenly, Rico turned his pistol toward Schmidt and fired. Schmidt darted a glance at Rico, but his eyes quickly became vacant and he slumped over. A large pool of blood stained his blue blazer and he lay still, unable to speak. The pistol fell out of his limp hand on to the floor mat.

Rico looked over at Sandoval and Montoya and nodded. They let go of Dennis, and he kneeled down next to Donna. He kissed the side of her swollen face and then took out the first aid kit from the kitchenette. Donna grimaced and let out a soft "ouch" as Dennis cleaned the cut with a cotton ball dipped in ethanol.

CHAPTER 16

SHALL WE DANCE?

It was late Sunday morning, a week after Easter. The bright sun lit up the room through the window at the University of Chicago Hospital where Donna Stevens was resting following the surgery she'd had on her right cheek bone several days before. She raised the hand-held mirror to examine her face. Other than a small bandage and some swelling, it didn't look too bad, she thought. She was ready to go home.

"You look great," Dennis smiled as he walked in. He approached the side of Donna's bed and hugged her lightly with his arms around her shoulders. Rico followed Dennis into the room, beaming. He was delighted to be part of the happy occasion.

"Thanks for coming to see me," Donna said to Rico, "and thank you for saving my life on the plane."

Rico nodded graciously. "It was dicey for a while—for everyone. Unfortunately, Schmidt couldn't be saved."

"What about Sandoval and Montoya?" Donna inquired. "What will happen to them?"

"They've been arrested and will be indicted, of course," Dennis answered, "but I don't think Klein will go heavy on them. After all, they didn't fight back after Schmidt was shot."

"That's a mitigating factor," Rico said. "I can testify that they turned on Schmidt and helped me to subdue him."

"What about Schmidt's body?" Donna asked. "What's going to happen to it?"

"As soon as the coroner releases it, we're going to ship it back to Argentina," Dennis replied.

"Ms. Atoche asked that he be buried at La Chacarita Cemetery in Buenos Aires," Rico added. "There is a section there for ethnic Germans."

"Rico and I will accompany the body to Argentina," Dennis said.

Donna glanced at Dennis. "How long do you plan to stay there?"

"I'm not sure," Dennis replied, looking back at Donna. "There are the funeral arrangements to be made and the burial itself. Also I want to spend some time with Mom and my brother Marko."

Dr. Benjamin Messner, the plastic surgeon who had operated on Donna, walked in with several resident doctors in tow. "You're looking good," he said, examining Donna's chart at the end of the bed. "I'm going to authorize your release today."

"How about the stitches?" Donna asked.

"They're self-dissolving," Dr. Messner answered. "You're all set."

A nurse's assistant walked in after the doctors left. "I'll help you dress," she said, drawing the curtain around Donna's bed. Dennis and Rico waited patiently on the other side.

"What about Schmidt's operations?" Donna asked, changing into her street clothes.

"Engstrom wants us to assess the situation," Dennis answered. "If any of them can be salvaged, we'll try to restructure them into something resembling a legitimate business."

Donna was silent while she continued to dress and collect her things.

"What about you?" Dennis asked. "What are your plans?"

"Hannigan asked me to join his campaign for governor," Donna responded. "I think I'll take him up on it."

Donna peered out from behind the bed curtain as the nurse's assistant zipped up the back of her dress.

Dennis's eyes were open wide as he looked back at Donna. "Can you take some time off and go with us to Argentina?" he asked.

The nurse's assistant drew back the curtain from around the bed. Donna walked up to Dennis. Dennis held her close and gave her a hug.

"Is that an invitation?" she asked.

"Yes," Dennis answered. "Besides," he added, "I'd like to learn how to do the tango."

"Buenos Aires is a beautiful city to visit," Rico jumped in. "You'll have time now to see Calle Florida, with the high-end boutiques from around the world."

The phone on the nightstand rang. Donna picked it up. It was Hannigan.

"How are you doing, tiger girl?" Hannigan asked cheerily.

"Much better, Mr. Hannigan," Donna replied. "Thank you for calling."

"Glad to hear that," Hannigan went on. "When are you coming back to help out with my campaign?"

"I need a few more weeks, Mr. Hannigan. The events of the past few days have taken a toll on me. I'd like to take a little vacation."

"Absolutely," Hannigan encouraged her. "Take all the time you need. What are your plans?"

"I was thinking about some R and R in Buenos Aires," Donna said.

Dennis, Donna, and Rico walked out into the hallway. "Can arrangements be made for us to take tango lessons in Buenos Aires?" Donna asked, turning to Rico.

"You don't need lessons," Rico replied with a smile. "You go to a small local club late in the evening, have a nice dinner, drink some Malbec wine, and then you just let the music take you."

Author Bio

Illinois attorney Tony Mankus focuses on tax controversies including tax collections, audits, and criminal investigations. He and his wife Margarita Marchan-Mankus are partners in the law firm of Mankus & Marchan, Ltd. They married in 1983 and have four grown daughters.

Tony joined the Peace Corps and worked as a revenue officer for the Internal Revenue Service before becoming an attorney. He earned his law degree from the John Marshall Law School in Chicago in 1985.

His literary background includes publishing both technical articles dealing with tax and bankruptcy issues and more personal and creative ones published in the Non-Billable Hours section of the Chicago Daily Law Bulletin, Lithuanian Heritage magazine, and Rivulets. He has also published a memoir, Where Do I Belong?, about his World War II experiences as a Lithuanian refugee displaced in Germany before immigrating to the United States. Find out more about Tony's immigrant experience at www.tonymankus.com.

Made in the USA
Lexington, KY
29 May 2016